E. Ca´

The Clockwork Tomb

Folley & Mallory

Copyright E. Catherine Tobler, 2017
ecatherine.com

cover by Ravven
ravven.com

isbn: 978-1547169450

Published by Apokrupha
apokrupha.com

Adventures of Folley and Mallory

The Rings of Anubis
The Glass Falcon
The Honey Mummy
The Clockwork Tomb
The Quartered Heart (Coming Soon!)

The Clockwork Tomb

Folley & Mallory

I.

At the bottom of the world, there runs a river.

Eleanor Folley stared, a curious blend of dismay and astonishment washing over her. She could see, perfectly reflected in the still black water, the outline of their falling bodies. Her hands were outstretched, thin fingers pale against the darkness. The reflection of Mallory's arms crisscrossed her own, his body somewhat behind hers. Above hers, she corrected, for they were falling from a very great height, to the center of the earth, it had to be.

Closer to the river, the sharper their reflected images became. There was nothing to grasp to forestall the fall—no rope, no ladder—and only a thin shower of sand clouding around them, it having slipped with them from the tomb's collapsing shale doorway. A doorway leading not into a room but into a pit that had no apparent sides, and a river at its lowest level. The sand preceded them to the river, spreading across the water as stardust might, Eleanor thought a second before she hit the river's black surface.

Eleanor knew better than to breathe—but she gasped in surprise, having thought the water would be warm, a slow umbilical running through the— The desert? The world? Duat? She gasped and drew black water into her mouth.

The river was not salty, nor was it sweet; it was the foulest thing she had ever tasted—even allowing that she had sampled Auberon's cooked eels. The water was thick as sludge against her tongue and though Eleanor was aware she was not breathing—was aware too of the hard smack and plunge of Mallory behind her as his body struck hers—she was desperate only to get the water out of her mouth. To have it stop touching her. Breath seemed the least of her worries as the water slithered over her. Into her.

The river seemed unlike water then. It moved in a way that water did not move—a knowing way—and Eleanor bucked in an effort to escape it. Mallory scrambled to do the same, but the water clung, and seeming possessed of hands—of claws—pulled them ever deeper into its black maw.

II.

Eleven Days Earlier

January 1890, the skies above Egypt

The *Jackal* flew through warming skies, leaving the chill of snow-draped Paris in its wake. Beneath the airship, Egypt spread golden and warm, sand undulating as an ocean might. Shadows made curious shapes of the sand, birds melting into pits, pits rising suddenly into monstrous mountains that curled over in waves, to cascade down long slopes where they pooled anew. January was the ideal season for digging, and Eleanor Folley had been promised a dig indeed.

On her room's balcony, sheltered from the Egyptian sun with a crescent-shaped canopy of blue, Eleanor looked again at the notebook Virgil Mallory had gifted her with the day before. Small and timeworn, its brown leather had been worn by familiar, worrying fingers. Familiar, for Eleanor had confirmed what Mallory believed, that the notes were made in her father's own hand. This was curious enough on its own, but the book had been found within Mistral's archive of largely-purloined goods. Eleanor could not explain it—how had Howard Irving come to possess an item belonging to her father? She told herself answers would come in time, but she was impatient.

The contents of the notebook were likewise baffling: her father had made incomplete notes on a tomb and its contents, neither of which seemed of any consequence. The tomb was small and if any other archaeologist had made study of it, thorough or otherwise, she and Mallory hadn't turned up a single shred of evidence. The only interesting thing about the tomb seemed to be its location, between KV 20, a tomb meant for Hatshepsut, and Hatshepsut's own mortuary temple east of the Valley of the Kings.

Eleanor got goosebumps to think what it might mean. Was the tomb connected to her mother's journey into eighteenth-dynasty Egypt during Hatshepsut's reign? It would have been easy enough to ask—her father was alive and well and working at his precious Nicknackatarium in Dublin, with Juliana Day at his side. But Eleanor did not ask, because her father had hidden too many things from her in the past. This felt precisely the same, and so she selfishly kept the notebook to herself, refusing to even tell her father Mallory had found it, and instead taking Mallory up on his offer of a journey to the tomb itself.

"Folley."

Mallory emerged carrying two cups of tea, steam still curling over the edge of each. The scent of Earl Grey, floral and citrus, carried to her and Eleanor eagerly took one cup from Mallory's chilled hands. She noticed the way they trembled, his body still fighting its addiction to opium. She did not ask how he was, knowing, when he held her gaze a little longer than necessary, that he was doing as well as could be expected. Eleanor sipped her tea and offered him a grin.

"You're quite overdue," he added, keeping his tea cupped

in his hands, though taking no sip of it yet.

Eleanor arched an eyebrow. "Me, overdue? Surely you're mistaken, Mallory. I am more timely than a clock—without the vexing chime at the top of every hour."

"Here I've gone to these lengths," Mallory said, his own mouth seeming to struggle with a grin. He gestured to the airship around them, then swept his hand outward from the balcony, as if to indicate the whole of Egypt below them. "Great and majestic lengths, mind you, and I've not a single thing in return."

"Thing," Eleanor murmured. She drank more tea and pondered the man before her.

He was still new to her—beautiful and strange and absolutely necessary to her life—and she had not tired of simply looking at him. His dark hair was ever-mussed, his teasing smile constantly crooked, and it seemed impossible she would *ever* tire. She loved looking for hints of the wolf beneath his skin, and loved even better when she found them in the sudden and golden gleam of a teasing eye, in toothy grins bestowed.

"I believe you should define this word, for I've given you a few things, indeed."

A toothy grin emerged at that and Eleanor's heart leaped to see it. She was as new to him as he was to her, and his eyes lingered too. She liked the way he took her in, perhaps remembering what she had of him—the evenings they had spent getting to better know one another. The excessively late evenings. Her cheeks warmed. No matter how much she did enjoy it, it was so new as to still be alarming. She had not had such a person in her life for a good many years.

"Here I believed New Year's gifts were all the rage—and I've gifted you with something potentially lavish indeed—that notebook in your father's own hand, leading us to a tomb he may well have explored. I daresay, I'm not sure how you mean to follow this up!"

Eleanor bit the inside of her cheek, trying not to laugh.

"I'm not certain, either," she said, exaggerating her despair. Indeed she did know, and had meant to gift him before he'd come to her with the notebook yesterday—the notebook that was so thoroughly astonishing, all thought of other gifts had gone from her mind. But now, in the air, she thought her actual gift would have to wait.

"There's something, well, *meager* in my coat pocket if you'd like to go digging."

It was Mallory's turn to arch a brow. "I do love to dig in your pockets," he said. He set his teacup and saucer on the balcony's rail, eying Eleanor's jacket with suspicion. "So many pockets."

Eleanor, keeping notebook in one hand and tea in the other, only lifted her arms so that Mallory might pat down every pocket her traveling coat possessed until he found the lump in the right pocket. His hands took a few detours, and she could not fault him this; if asked to search his pockets, she was quite certain her route would have also been compromised.

"This is smaller than a tomb," he murmured, sliding his hand into the pocket.

"Indeed, it's a rare woman who can conceal an entire tomb in her pockets—given the dire state of lady's pockets as a whole. But you should not be entirely too displeased—after all, it is a token from my heart, Mallory—small and easily carried next to your own, meager though such a gift may seem."

Mallory grunted, more than a hint of the wolf in the sound, and Eleanor grinned as he withdrew the brown velvet pouch from her pocket. He lifted it by its golden strings, tied prettily around the bag's mouth in a generous bow. A small tag upon the strings said *For Mallory, for always.*

"Always is rather a long time, Folley," he said, but his face lost the tension it had held, smoothing into something becalmed, as if she had stroked a slow hand over his wolfish head.

"Not for what's inside," she said and lowered her arms. She slid the notebook into the vacated jacket pocket, and leaned upon the airship's rail, watching as he jostled the bag in an attempt to discern its contents. "You really were the most fastidious child on Christmas mornings, weren't you?"

"I assure you, I still am."

The objects inside made a soft clinking sound, though not loud enough to reveal their precise nature. They might have been anything, seeming only a child's toy based on their lumps through the bag. Mallory untied the tag, slipping it into his own jacket pocket before he untied the strings and spread the mouth of the velvet bag wide. Once tipped, a trio of gilded nutmegs tumbled into his palm.

"*Tesorina.*"

Mallory's mouth was warm on Eleanor's before she expected it. He tasted like tea, but beneath the gentle warmth was the reminder that a beast lurked within. His teeth nipped her bottom lip and she curled a hand into his hair, to keep him right where he was, for minutes that were more than strictly necessary.

"Here, you've given me something beautifully symbolic of continued wealth and prosperity," Mallory said, "and I...I've given you a yawning pit of gloom within the earth that leads to God only knows what."

"*Also* beautifully symbolic." Eleanor gently nudged her shoulder into his. "Riches and wealth beyond the telling, I would imagine—and honestly, a journal belonging to my father? Priceless. Worth more than three golden nut—"

Mallory's mouth over hers again silenced her and Eleanor savored it, unable to keep from smiling when Mallory hauled her closer, closer where he smelled like tea and soap. The only casualty in the embrace was the teacup Mallory had placed on the rail; as his arm came more fully around Eleanor, his elbow knocked into the cup, sending it and its saucer plummeting to the desert below.

"Oh, that was a matched pair," Mallory murmured when he lifted his mouth from Eleanor's. Eleanor, still holding her own cup of tea, took a final sip before allowing hers to likewise sail into the sands below. "Oh, Folley, you're a romantic."

"Don't tell me you're not."

The wind-sculpted desert was something of a second home to Eleanor and she leaned against Mallory, to watch it pass beneath them. Their pilot, the indefatigable Gin, was bringing them straight across the Valley of the King's, south and east toward the rise that concealed the marvels of Deir el-Bahri. They had explored those halls and colonnades, though Eleanor longed to return. She had once questioned her life's work—if being the child of archaeologists meant she had to be one too, but the dust of Egypt had been rubbed into her at a young age, and it had yet to fade. Beyond her parents' work, she wanted to understand the ancient world, and preserve what she might, before time could wash the secrets away.

Above them, the airship's radio crackled to life, though whatever Gin said was lost in a scattering of static. *The Jackal* was, however, losing altitude, skimming low above the valley of tombs, toward its eastern edge. This low, Eleanor could see the murky doorways and paler pathways leading into the final resting places of Egypt's nobility. Each gave her a thrill, but they bypassed them all, heading for KV20 and the land that spread beyond. KV20, known to even Napoleon, had once been reserved for Hatshepsut herself; the tomb beyond it was, according to her father's notes, greatly unknown, insignificant, a nothing. And yet, her father had devoted an entire notebook to it.

"Oh, there—you can see its door," Mallory said, and pointed toward a shadowed hump amid the hard stone and blown sand. "It really does look like precisely nothing, unless you're actually looking for it." Sand had drifted cross the cut entry, clear indication that no one had visited in many months, if not longer.

A glorified hole in the ground, her father had called it in his notes; a minor tomb of little significance, and yet.

"Virgil." Eleanor's hand tightened on his arm as the airship drew closer and Gin prepared to set them down. "Do you think—" Her throat tightened and she could not finish until Mallory clasped her hand in return. "It was my grandmother we found in the sands, after all—not my mother. Do you think my father was still looking for her, even after he asked me to stop? She was buried somewhere—had she fled with my grandmother, surely we would have..." But the desert was vast, and finding one body did not mean they would find another even closely by.

"Do I think it's your mother's tomb?" Mallory's hand tightened around Eleanor's, warm and strong. His thumb stroked over her own. "I don't know and given what we discovered of both her and your grandmother, I would not wager a guess. However, given the tomb's proximity to a tomb intended for Hatshepsut and, and to Deir el-Bahri itself, I would call us fools if we didn't suspect a connection. Your father doesn't mention connections in the journal, but then, he also never told you your mother planned her journey to the ancient world. I'm not certain he's been forthcoming about much, nor perhaps would he want his papers to be forthcoming."

I meant to say goodbye, Eleanor. Her mother's words remained close at hand, spoken in the still-thriving gardens of Deir el-

Bahri thousands of years ago, and yet also only three months before. Eleanor had crossed time to hear those words, to understand what had happened to her mother when she herself was only a child; accepting it was another thing entirely—though Eleanor felt she was nearly there. She understood what it was to love this land so well; understood what it was to give herself wholly to it.

"If the tomb is my mother's," Eleanor said, "this had damned well better be it—the end, no more. I'm done chasing her ghost. She gave up this life for another—and I won't chase my tail—literal and not—in order to bring her back. She doesn't want to come back, and truth be told, I'd rather she not be here. She is happier there, so be it. Not that I'm ungrateful for your gift…never that. But some ghosts need rest."

Mallory pressed a gentle kiss against Eleanor's temple as *The Jackal* made its final descent. The airship carried a crew of two, in addition to Gin, and the new recruits were in charge of anchoring the airship. This involved the discharge of an anchor into the hard-packed earth, after which, Miss Wise and Mister Gathright slithered down rope ladders, securing *The Jackal* to the trio of metal cleats that had long ago been sunk into the desert ground for such purposes. The solution had come from long and fierce battles between those who wanted to raise an airship station in the desert and those who refused to see the pristine valley ruined by such a blight—as had Paris been ruined with Eiffel's tower, many said. Mallory had snorted an agreement to that, and Eleanor had silently agreed; to see such a structure raised within the Valley of the Kings would have altered too much.

It was a good first mission for the young agents, Eleanor thought; simple and direct, unlike Mistral's usual. Ferry agents to a tomb for leisurely explorations? Anchor an airship? Easy and done, and Wise and Gathright would have time for disasters later.

"Two days?" Gin asked, peeling his goggles from his face. The young man was thin, his reddish hair caught back in the sloppy queue he seemed to favor. Eleanor thought squirrels helped him dress in the mornings, his clothes were so rumpled. Today, he did not smell of fried fish, but of fried eels and Eleanor despaired to think that Auberon's snack had captured a wider appreciation. "Back for you on Thursday the tenth."

Perhaps squirrels managed his calendars as well. "Being that today is Monday the sixth, two days is Wednesday the eighth," she said. "You're going to forget entirely about us, aren't you—carousing in Luxor—and we'll be left to the desert wastes, to the jackals."

"At least we'll have an in with them," Mallory murmured, before stepping away to collect their gear for tomb exploration.

Did her nature, given that Eleanor was part jackal, allow her an affinity with other jackals? If they were not also human, she supposed not, but part of her was now eager to see if she could speak to the animals—and they to her.

"Do you have many conversations with wolves then, Mallory?" she asked as he offered her the leather pack she had not carried in far too many years. The pack had been a good friend to her in countless tombs, a gift from her father. Eleanor knew its weight and shape and it seemed to know her, the soft browned leather settling against her back as she strapped it on. It contained most of what they would need inside the tomb, save for the small hammer she hefted and slid through a ring on her belt.

"They don't say much worthwhile," Mallory said, handing Eleanor a goat-skin bag filled with water, "and before you say the same of *me*, tell me if you can handle two canteens, to be safe."

"Before you liken me to a camel, yes," Eleanor said.

Gin hooted with laughter as they continued to collect their gear. Mallory possessed a pack similar to her own, having outfitted it at her instruction: food, ropes, a compass; gloves, a magnifying glass, a knife; a foldable shovel, brushes, paper, and charcoal pencils. Rope, a grappling hook, and an unloaded revolver with a small box of ammunition. One never knew.

"We won't let him forget you," Miss Wise promised as Eleanor and Mallory set foot into the desert, still framed within the airship's shadow. It was nearing noon, but given it was January, the air was still comfortable.

"And if he does," Mallory said, eyeing Gin, Miss Wise, and Mister Gathright speculatively, "be sure the headlines are grand. Pair Forced to Endure Hike from Valley of Kings to Luxor's Mighty Gates; Welcomed By Rain, Hailed Heroes."

"Have you ever explored a tomb, Mallory?" Eleanor asked as *The Jackal* took to the sky once more, headed toward the Nile where Luxor awaited them. Wise and Gathright loosened the mooring lines from the cleats, then slithered up the trailing ropes and into the ship's belly, even as she had begun to move off. They were like acrobats, Eleanor thought, the ship grand from even the ground, windsails trailing in her wake. She was bronze and cream and gleaming, silent as she turned her sharp face into the afternoon breeze.

Mallory adjusted the strap on his bag, then unfolded his shovel. "I have not. I trust it won't be painful."

Eleanor hefted the as-yet unlit fanous, which would see them through countless dark corridors, and turned toward the tomb's entrance. Her father's journal felt like a heavy stone in her pocket; was it her mother's tomb? Impossible. "Oh, but some of the best things are painful, aren't they?"

They shared a moment's silence—each knew this was true—then Eleanor moved toward the entry, Mallory carving them a path through the sand drifts with his shovel. As he worked, Eleanor lit the lantern. The four sides of the fanous were fitted with glass windows, in turn covered with cut metal panels that could be manipulated to direct the light where one needed. Eleanor left the panels open for the time being, the light blooming outward to pierce the tomb's entry. As other tombs, it was closed with a door of stone and Eleanor didn't know if they'd be able to open it at all; some doors had required levers and pulleys to be opened, the Egyptians having wanted to secure their royals for eternity.

As always, Eleanor got a chill as she stood before the doors. She pictured who had stood here centuries before, sealing the doors. Who had carved them, for upon the limestone she could make out hieroglyphs, speaking to Ra, and eternity, and the vault of heaven above. There was no name, but this was not in any way odd; had there been a stelae, it would have contained the name, but Eleanor saw no such marker. If there had ever been one, any evidence of it had been worn away in the desert winds.

"This tomb wasn't robbed?" she asked, stepping closer to run her fingers over the stone. It was gritty with sand, and warm despite the shadows that cloaked it.

"Not according to your father's notes," Mallory said, "but those notes are countless years old." He lifted the shovel, allowing the last shovelful of sand to cascade from its tip before he folded it away. "I'm still not sure if your father explored the tomb or not—some of those notes are cryptic indeed."

"A riddle," Eleanor said—for even if the journal were found, her father might not want its contents known. She curled her hand around the door's broad handle. But she could not move the weight of the door one bit and she grunted. Even setting the lantern aside and pulling with both hands did nothing to move the massive limestone.

"Here." Mallory joined her, grasping the other side of the handle with both hands. Together, they pulled and the door felt neither heavy nor stuck; to Eleanor's surprise, it moved as if on wheels. "Brilliant."

Warm, stale air rushing from the tomb lifted Eleanor's hair from her cheeks and neck. Eleanor knew many archaeologists had grown ill after exploring closed tombs, but she smelled nothing strange or toxic; it was only as it might be opening a room one had closed after, appropriately, a death. No one had been here in a long time.

Eleanor took the lantern back up, while Mallory wedged a sliver of stone beneath the entry door. The open door did not allow much light to enter, but the fresher air was welcome as they walked deeper into the entry corridor. The limestone flooring beneath their boots was slick with sand, but largely undisturbed; there was no sign that robbers had found this corridor, for the walls were whole, coated in sand and dust. The walls were not carved with text, but stood smooth and nearly flawless. In the softly diffuse lamplight, Eleanor could not see more than a few paces before them and walked slowly, wanting to be sure the ground remained firm underfoot.

"Oh, Virgil, it's breathtaking."

Mallory ran a hand over the nearest wall, disturbing the layer of dust and sand. "Are you certain? There's nothing here. Not a single, solitary mark. Not even of a tool..."

Eleanor continued down the straight, unadorned corridor, listening to Mallory behind her. "Nothing is quite something, given how Egyptians loved to decorate their tombs."

The corridor remained straight and flat, the lantern's light spreading in a golden bubble around them. She lifted the light, to find the ceiling close above them. She could reach out and press her hand flat against it, the stone still unmarred. Beneath her hand, it was as gritty as sun-warmed pear skin.

"Not even painted as a night sky...is that why the robbers ignored it, because it was so plain?"

"Or they couldn't open that damned heavy door," Mallory offered.

When at last the corridor veered, it made a ninety-degree turn to the north. The walls felt impossibly close and perhaps it was an effect of the low ceiling too, but Eleanor found herself taking deeper breaths, for it felt as though the walls were closing in. When the plain corridor righted itself again, it turned east once more, the corridor narrow enough to force Eleanor and Mallory to walk single file.

"There."

Ahead in the dim light, a shape on the ground made itself known. At the touch of Mallory's hand upon her shoulder, Eleanor stopped walking, mindful that the shadowed lump might be anything. She drew in a deep breath and heard Mallory do the same, but they both shook their heads.

"Not living then," Mallory said, and together, they crept closer.

The lump revealed itself to be a body, the flesh withered down to the bones, which were still draped in tattered clothing. Short cropped hair, trousers, and laced leather boots told them it had been a man, but the flesh was too far gone to tell anything else. He looked whole and undisturbed, the desert heat having made a mummy of him, but for the rusted spike protruding from his temple. The long spike had shattered the skull in a neat hole, pinning the man to the ground. What had once been a blood pool beneath him was now ruddy powder, blood turned nearly to sand.

"That's..." Eleanor frowned at the body.

"Gruesome?" Mallory asked.

Eleanor offered Mallory the lantern so she could explore the walls. They remained smooth and without decoration; no paint, no hieroglyphs, no hidden tubes where such spikes might explode from. Not that she expected *those*—they would have been strange, indeed.

"Egyptians don't trap their tombs that way," she said as she stepped past the body, placing it between herself and Mallory. She looked at Mallory in the lantern light, then back to the mummy at their feet. "They certainly did trap them, but, stakes that shoot from the walls? Entirely fictional. This man was murdered."

"With some great force, I'd say," Mallory said. "I don't see footprints—and given the condition of the body...how long does it take flesh to wither?"

"In desert heat? Trapped in a tomb?" Eleanor shook her head. "Not long at all." She kneeled before the body and grunted softly. "Do forgive me," she whispered, then gently patted down the man's trouser pockets. Each was, however, empty, and so too his jacket pockets. Other than his boot laces, the body held nothing of value. "A quarrel between robbers after all?"

Mallory stepped over the body, carrying the lantern some paces away, farther down the corridor. "There's a turn here—it keeps going. Shall we?"

Eleanor stood and withdrew her father's notebook, unable to stop herself before she slanted a smile at Mallory. "The body only makes it more interesting, don't you think? Leaving now tells us nothing—and it was already dangerous, even without...him." She looked at the body, shivering despite the warmth in the corridor. Part of her could not help but question if the body was that of her own father, even though she knew it was absolutely not. Still, having unearthed her own grandmother...Eleanor opened the notebook. The pages stuck together, however, the sound of ripping paper surprisingly loud within the tomb.

"Oh, blast."

Eleanor stopped opening the book, but saw then how the pages were stuck, how they had been folded together. She blew into the book in an effort to separate the pages, sliding her finger into a small gap when it opened enough so as to do no more damage.

"Oh Virgil—it's a map."

The pages unfolded to reveal a map of the tomb, the corridor they presently stood in clearly marked. The lines showed nothing extraordinary—corridors snaking back on one another, and the sketch of a chamber some feet away from the corridor itself—the notes alongside still in her father's hand.

"So he *was* here," Mallory said.

Eleanor exhaled. "We carry on then, see if we can find this chamber." She touched the square and read the words beside it: *no key*.

"No key," Eleanor said as they continued down the corridor, Mallory preceding her this time. In his shadow, she could not read the journal, so tucked it away, content to see

19

how the tomb unfolded on its own. "What on earth would he have been looking for?"

"Maybe it's not so complex," Mallory said, hefting the lantern as they turned down another sharp corner, and yet another. "Perhaps he didn't know—if he lacked a key, perhaps he got no further than that chamber. Perhaps he— Oh."

They turned down another corridor and peering over Mallory's shoulder, Eleanor saw the reason for his dismayed exclamation. A dead end.

"Oh," Eleanor echoed.

She pushed carefully past Mallory, for the corridor ended in a false door, not another blank wall. She spread her hands on the carving, finding it exquisite, despite being crusted with sand and dust. It was otherwise unbroken.

Like any other false door, it was a single slab of stone, carved with a series of door frames upon its face, one layered inside the other to mark a slow progression inward, as if toward a final passage. Each was inscribed with hieroglyphs, but as Eleanor fingered the sand from them, she felt a little sick at what they spelled out. There was no name, no royal station or wishes for the next life, only a persistent warning to not enter.

"Folley?"

"It bids one not to enter," she said, "but it is a false door." She eyed the stone as Mallory stepped closer, examining the hieroglyphs himself. "It isn't a door meant to open, so—"

But even as she spoke, Mallory touched the stone as she touched the stone, fingering a line of sand from the words, and

Eleanor felt the stone *move* beneath their hands. Eleanor jerked her hands back as though she had been burned.

"Did you feel it move?" she whispered.

"Yes, but no longer." Mallory put his hand flush against the stone and pushed, but the stone was resolute, unmoving.

"It isn't *meant* to open," Eleanor said, as if arguing with nature itself. Refusing to touch the stone, she withdrew her father's notebook again and carefully opened it, to the map they had discovered. The chamber was shown some distance from the end of the corridor in which they stood—the end being the false door? Eleanor could not tell, but those words—*no key*.

"If it isn't meant to open," Mallory said, looking at Eleanor over the lantern as he set it down before the door, "and yet it does...does that mean it might also make use of a key, when such a door normally would not?"

"Perhaps?" Eleanor could not quite distance herself from the sensation of the stone moving beneath their hands. False doors did not move because they were false. They were not hinged, they did not lead anywhere, only existed as a symbol for the spirit moving on to the next life, through doorways untold, to—

She watched as Mallory went to his knees, rooting through the thin layer of sand upon the floor. Handfuls of sand revealed no key, however; no little bit of metal that would fit— Where? Eleanor saw no lock within the slab of stone, either, no place where a key would normally fit, and yet, the door had moved. Under their paired hands, exactly as the first door had.

"Mallory, there's no key—not as we know it. Come—put your hands on the stone with mine."

Eleanor pressed her hands flat against the stone, disregarding the words of warning beneath. Mallory straightened and did the same, his hands outside hers upon the outermost carved frame. Their hands looked like doorways of a sort, she thought—larger on the outside, smaller on the inside, and when the door did not move, she bit out a curse.

"If it's not—"

But as she spoke, the stone moved beneath their hands. Eleanor sucked in a breath and could not reason how such a thing was possible. False doors did not move, but this one did, sliding inward on protesting gears to reveal blackness beyond. It did not move as smoothly as the outer door had, sand gritting beneath its heavy edge. The lantern light did little to penetrate it, the air beyond thick and stale with heat.

"We're the key?" Mallory whispered.

"If my father came alone, he wouldn't have gotten far, unless there's another mummy elsewhere in this—"

Eleanor grew silent, as far behind them up the long corridor, the entry door sucked itself shut. The air rushed from the chamber they had opened, warm and foul, stirring the sand into a cloud between them. The sound of the tomb door closing far and away was hideous, the long howl of a trapped monster, and Eleanor's entire body seemed to bristle. She lifted her hands from the false door and it ceased its movement. Mallory plucked the lantern from the floor, moving the metal panels until he could thrust a single stream of light into the darkness ahead.

"Still onward, Folley?"

It was something in his voice, a slight hesitation even as he lifted the lamp and looked beyond where they stood. The lantern flickered as his hand shook, and whether it was the lack of opium that was troubling him or something else, Eleanor reminded herself that Mallory had not explored tombs, that this was his first. Everyone reacted differently, and the body they'd found couldn't have helped the experience. She glanced back at the body, now nearly invisible as the shadows closed over it.

"Still onward. You know, Petrie took us to Giza when I was a child," Eleanor told Mallory as they passed through the doorway, hoping her steady voice would ease any concerns he had the deeper they walked into the tomb. "The entrance into the pyramid was like a black rectangle cut from the night sky. I could not stand it inside—wanted only to be back out under the stars. My father told me everyone is afraid of something—even my parents—and lord, that didn't help."

Mallory laughed low, and reached back to take her hand and keep it folded inside his own. "It feels like a church in here—quiet and at peace somehow. I didn't expect that."

His hand was warm and steady now, gritty with sand, and Eleanor glanced at the false door behind them. It had not moved. Would it close as the one above them had, with no hands upon its hard face? As unsettling as the tomb had been, she wanted to venture on and understand the tomb, unlike any she had seen before. Even when she felt the limestone floor give way beneath them—even as the sand began to slide and they with it—she wanted to venture on.

III.

"Well that's butter on bacon."

In the warm dark, Eleanor laughed. "An apt assessment, Mallory."

She looked above them, but could see nothing. The blackness was unbroken, though the longer she looked, the more likely her eyes were to invent patterns as she struggled to see anything. The lantern had extinguished itself quite thoroughly upon their landing, but she hadn't heard it shatter, so took that as a good sign. Given the strangeness they had encountered so far, she would take an unbroken lantern.

"The lantern doesn't feel broken," Mallory said, as if anticipating her questions.

Eleanor sat up slowly, sand whispering out of her blouse and the cuffs of her trousers. She and Mallory sat atop more sand, and experimentally, Eleanor explored where they had fallen. She carefully pushed her hands into the sand, searching for spikes, bones, or anything that might had been made to rudely welcome them to the pit, but she encountered only sand.

"And you, Mallory?"

"I seem whole as well."

Mallory struck flint against steel, and threw the profusion of sparks toward the lantern's candle. The sparks caught, and he moved the metal panels to further flood the small chamber with a warm light that called to mind sunrise. Eleanor looked about in an effort to gauge where they'd landed, but the room gave little away. The chamber was no more than four feet square; with the lantern burning, she could see high above them, the small opening they'd fallen through barely a shadow in the wall.

"We can possibly reach it with the grappling," Mallory said.

"Possibly," Eleanor said, though her attention shifted back to the chamber. The walls here were not smooth like the corridor had been, but were written upon at great length—much like the false door, the words told them to turn back.

"Whosoever shall continue onward," she read aloud, "shall meet that which should not be met." Eleanor eyed Mallory.

"I thought we needed a sphinx for proper riddles." Mallory struggled to his feet, but he promptly sank into the sand, unable to stand on its surface. The sand whispered against his trousers, small eddies working within the grains. He braced a hand against one wall. "Does quicksand exist in Egypt, Folley?"

Eleanor's heart leapt. "Trust you to gift me with the most curious tomb in the neighborhood." She tried to stand as well, but her boots sank, the sand seeming to tangle itself in her boot laces in a concerted effort to pull her down. "It's not wet—it's not quicksand, it's..." But she had no ready explanation for it—or for the entire tomb—and stared at Mallory, willing herself not to panic. "I said Egyptians didn't trap their tombs with flying spikes and bolts, but they were quite well-versed in using the desert to foil robbers."

The sand pulled harder and swallowed Eleanor to her knees. She pulled the straps on her pack tighter, ensuring she had both canteens as well. She pushed herself forward, through the rapidly shifting sand, toward Mallory.

"The thing about this sand is—" As if the sand heard her, it pulled on Eleanor a little more firmly. She lunged for Mallory and he grasped her by the arm, hauling her closer. "It's going somewhere—can you feel it? Egyptians did use sand falls, so when we reach the next chamber—" *Let there be another chamber!* she thought—"we need to move quickly. If *this* sand fills *that* room—"

It could mean there were sharpened spears at the bottom of this chamber after all, she thought but did not say. The sand would flood out of this chamber and into the next and they would be carried along, as fish in a stream, she prayed.

"Hold on to me *and* the lantern. Don't let either go. You need both to make it through this tomb. The lantern will go out, but hold to it."

Eleanor flashed a smile, even as the sand increased its hold upon them; she did not believe Mallory would leave her behind, only knew that being separated would not increase their chances of survival.

They were sinking, the sand beginning to cover thighs and hips. Even so, Eleanor studied the chamber's walls. Each was maddeningly identical, giving no clue as to where any doorway might be. They might end up wedged against a wall with no exit, the sand packing over them. They might suffocate against the floor, only steps from the proper outlet.

They might—

The sand gave way with a sound of rushing water. There was no warning, only a golden spiral of sand that hauled them down. Eleanor held hard to Mallory, lacing her fingers through his, and saw only determination writ upon his face as the rushing air extinguished the lantern. In the warm, whirling darkness, the sand was like a thousand birds whirling in angry flight. Eleanor thought there would have been more confusion, that she would have lost her sense of up and down, but down was readily apparent, the sand pulling hard upon her legs, as if it were possessed of hands. Eleanor held her breath and didn't dare open her eyes; the sand slid into her jacket collar and down her blouse, burrowed into her hair, and pressed against her cheeks. In the mad rush, she was keenly aware of Mallory's hand within hers, his fingers locked as tightly as her own.

And then, he was gone, ripped into the draining sand.

Eleanor cried out, sand plastering itself against her tongue. Eleanor dragged her arm sand-weighted arm over her face, but could still not open her eyes; the force of the sand and wind kept her as she was, shut up and away and ever falling. It was endless until the world narrowed. The sand tapered around her body, pulling in tight, and Eleanor waited for the thump of her boots against floor, or the squelch of a spear in her side. Neither came. The world grew darker, and her lungs shrieked for a clean breath. But then she felt it, a sloping ramp beneath her bottom, and she was sliding, until she emerged head over heel into a new chamber, sprawled inelegantly and spitting sand.

"Mallory!"

The chamber was pitch black and she had no good idea where Mallory or the lantern had landed. If they had landed.

"Virg—"

The lantern rolled into her head and Eleanor scrambled, pushing herself upright. Sand poured from her jacket and blouse, Eleanor pulling the latter from her belt to aid its escape. She could not tell if the sand was still filling the room, if they needed to find another exit, so struggled to pull her own flint and steel from her jacket pocket. It was wrapped where she'd left it and though the sparks briefly blinded her, she carefully lit the lantern and set it upright. A pair of wide golden eyes gleamed at her and she leapt back with a shriek. In the uneven lantern light, Mallory's brindled wolf sat before her, sand cascading from his fur. His nose twitched.

"Oh!"

Eleanor could not stop the laugh that bubbled up and the wolf ducked his head, as if embarrassed. Eleanor took a quick look around the chamber in which they found themselves, relieved to see the sand that had forced them here had dwindled to a trickle through the rough-cut doorway. She pondered the mechanisms at play, if within the shaft another door had closed, and if now that they had triggered the room to give way, the sand would be replenished.

She looked back at wolf Mallory, deciding there were other matters in need of tending first. "You know, jackals are partial to tombs—dead bodies and all. I'm not sure many wolves have toured the Valley of the Kings, Mallory. We could be making history here."

Mallory shifted from paw to paw and growled low in his throat. Eleanor eased her pack off, letting the canteens follow. Once these were carefully set aside, she unbuttoned her jacket and blouse, taking both off at once. At this, Mallory canted his head, eyes keenly observing not the sand Eleanor shook from her clothes, but the gleam of lamplight upon her bared skin. In only her camisole, Eleanor watched him in return.

"Unless you packed clothing, we should find yours, hmm?" She draped her blouse and jacket atop her pack, and began a search of the room, finding Mallory's clothing one article at a time; his jacket, shirt, and trousers were all torn, but would do, given the alternative. His boots were thrown against the far wall, full of sand. Likewise his pack, which she found in a puddle, for one of his canteens had ruptured.

"One casualty," she said, returning to the lantern, where wolf Mallory spat a sock into the pile of clothing. She spread the canteen out, but saw no good way it might be repaired, not with their current supplies.

She knew it was only a matter of time before Mallory came back to his human self—while temperament often governed the change, they'd been working to get a better handle on such matters. Still, anger and fear and stronger emotions could force one into their alternate shape, and one needed to grow calm before one could return. She made an effort to hold to her calm, not wanting to tour the tomb as a jackal.

Eleanor retrieved a canteen, and rinsed her own mouth out, before dribbling water into her hand so that Mallory could drink. He did so with long, slow licks, eventually tonguing her palm dry. Eleanor smiled at him, then saw beyond his bristled shoulder where something sparked in the darkness. She did not move, but Mallory was aware of the change within her: shoulders pulled tight, eyes unblinking. He ducked his head and Eleanor gave him a slow stroke between the ears, allowing him to dip his head and glance behind him. She hoped it looked perfectly natural to whatever might be watching them.

The lantern's light did not reach to the chamber's far wall, leaving a sizable portion of the room in gloom. This darkness was whole, as unpierced as the Egyptians had left it after carving the tomb. Beyond the golden circle of light that encompassed her and Mallory, something still wavered as if with reflected lantern light. In another place, Eleanor might have thought it was a doorknob. The shape was indistinct and Eleanor could not tell exactly how far away it was, but Mallory, still in wolf form, rose and loped into the black.

"Blast," Eleanor whispered, but did not stop him. Chances were, whatever it was certainly wouldn't be expecting to encounter a wolf.

Eleanor got to her feet and grabbed the lantern, following at a distance. She could not see Mallory, the darkness having swallowed him whole. The lantern spread its light, slowly revealing the chamber's far wall, a neatly cut doorway in its approximate center. A corridor extended far beyond the doorway, a corridor Mallory loped back up, alone.

"Not a hunting beast then," she said, and touched her

finger to his nose.

Eleanor shook her blouse out a final time, and pulled it back on, watching as Mallory gave himself up to the task of reverting to his human form. She shuddered a little to see it, though knew her body capable of the same. The process looked gruesome and sounded worse, bone and muscle shifting from one shape into the other. Mallory would be hungry and thirsty, and she hoped their supplies would see them through. They had not planned on such misadventures, and she rather doubted they would find their proper way out before Gin arrived to retrieve them.

"It's too bad we can't wire Gin for fresh supplies," Eleanor said, holding his trousers up. She could see the lamplight straight through their tattered lengths.

"I've worn worse," he said, pushing himself to sitting before he sucked long swallows of water from the skin. When he'd finished drinking, he stood to pull on his shirt, it hanging frayed against his slim hips. "In fact, there was one evening involving only my necktie—which I should probably not share with ladies, even if they are you."

"*Only* your necktie?" Eleanor handed the trousers over, and took the canteen in exchange, so that Mallory might pull on the fabric that remained. "This sounds like a story one will be required to share eventually."

"Sharing that which should not be shared," Mallory said, evoking the words they had read on the walls in the chamber above. "Do you think whatever you saw is that which should not be met?" He fastened his trousers and patted them down, a cloud of dust nearly swallowing him. "I didn't smell a damned thing, nor did I see much beyond an infinite corridor."

"I think whatever I saw will either reveal itself in time, or it won't. It might be as simple as a cobra—" But she laughed and shook her head. "Simple. But the desert has its own dangers remember—it doesn't have to be designed danger. Cool tombs like these? Cobras seek them for shelter, which means we might also find water."

"That tells me there are ways out, we have only to find them," Mallory said. "Aren't most tombs straightforward? Tricks a plenty, but the path does take one to what they seek? Those who made these tunnels also needed a way out, didn't they?"

"Oh, that depends," Eleanor said. "Some tomb builders gave up their lives in the building of the tombs. They needed no way out, for dying in their king's tomb was the ultimate sacrifice. Following them into the afterlife. That fellow up there"—Eleanor gestured above them, thinking of the first corridor and its body—"tells us someone was here and the behavior of the tomb tells us something else."

"That he likely had a partner," Mallory said. "Or perhaps more than one—whoever killed him could not have passed that initial door without assistance, which means we may yet find other bodies."

"Indeed so—and if we don't? They may well have gotten out."

The idea was encouraging, though Eleanor allowed something might be trapped within the tomb's black tunnels without having discovered a way out. Something mortal? Something deadly? Her thoughts flickered to Anubis and his fellow gods, trespassing where they would in the modern world. But Cleopatra also came to mind, the queen having cursed herself with immortality, only to spend her eternity within Alexandria's catacombs, mourning Antony who had never joined her, dead before their plan came to pass.

Mallory, having gathered the rest of their scattered gear, joined Eleanor at the lantern once more. She peered up at him, thoughtful of what might lay ahead.

"I'm going to suggest we camp here, Mallory. Eat, rest, and then head deeper." She nodded toward the singular doorway. "If anything is down here, we're in a defensible position—it's unlikely anyone will come from above."

"And if they do, we'll sure as hell hear them."

Mallory had overseen the food for the journey and handed Eleanor a somewhat squashed sandwich wrapped in paraffin paper. She unwrapped it, delighted to find crusty wheat bread, roasted beef—and entirely mangled tomatoes. The fruit had been smashed into near oblivion, leaving Mallory to wince.

"There are meat pies, too—if you'd rather?" But Eleanor had already bitten into the sandwich and she shook her head at Mallory. "Tinned sardines?" Another headshake. "Sweet pie?"

Eleanor lifted an eyebrow at that. "Oh, yes—later. This sandwich is perfectly fine, as it contains a precise rendering of your bottom in its bread."

"My—" Mallory broke off, laughter filling the small chamber.

He set his own smashed sandwich aside to offer Eleanor the canteen so that she might drink. She did, aware his eyes remained on her the entire time. "Your human bottom, perhaps I should clarify."

"You still surprise me, Miss Folley."

Eleanor wiped her mouth dry and offered the canteen back, brushing Mallory's sand-dusted hands as she did. "And you me," she said.

It did not take much encouragement to remember all the ways he had surprised her of late—though she would be hard-pressed to list them in any kind of tidy order. When she had only known Virgil Mallory for a Mistral agent—a mere four months prior—she had thought the most terrible things of him, thinking him one of the faceless agents with their own agendas of power and control. But Mallory's goals had proved aligned with her own. They both possessed a keen desire to see the ancient world preserved even as the modern world marched on.

Perhaps what surprised her most was the way in which Mallory always and constantly accepted her as she was—and beyond that, sought to see her flourish. Their increasingly intimate relationship did not surprise her, for who would not wish to spend such hours with a person who accepted them wholly as they were? There was nearly nothing so intoxicating, for Mallory was like a tomb himself, opening by degrees, allowing her to discover chambers and niches heretofore unknown. As she did for him.

The meal was one of the roughest they had known of late, but Eleanor found something magical in the sharing of food and water by sputtering lantern light. Perhaps it hearkened back to her childhood, cherished memories of leaping from tomb to tomb with her parents, or perhaps it stood well enough on its own, delightful in its own right, for exactly what it was. When Eleanor curled into Mallory's side in an attempt to rest, she tangled her fingers with his, listening to his own breathing even and slow. He leaned against the tomb wall, his arm curved around her as the lantern's light jumped.

"Rest, Folley—the way that light is dancing, we'll be out in no time. There's an air current somewhere close, aye?"

Somewhere close, she thought, and her eyes slid shut. It was not the first tomb she would sleep in, nor likely the last. She allowed herself to drift, feeling Mallory's mouth press against her forehead as her breath deepened.

She woke to the familiar sound of bats, leathery wings flapping against the tomb walls. In the lantern light, they were little more than shadows against the limestone, and then nothing at all as they spiraled up into the solid darkness of the shaft. By the time she and Mallory had broken their camp and prepared to head down the corridor, the bats had reappeared, flying against the corridor's ceiling, as Mallory hefted the lantern. He angled the metal pieces to direct the light down the corridor, the limestone walls gleaming and gold.

The walls here were not marked with warnings or otherwise, and as Mallory had joked, seemed to stretch forever. Eleanor saw no sign of snakes in the sand that scattered the floor; the sand, in fact, looked entirely undisturbed but for the bat guano they encountered deeper in. As the creatures swooped and flew to and fro, Eleanor found herself wishing for a pith helmet draped with a veil, for she had no desire to find a bat tangled in her hair.

"You don't suppose it's bats all the way down, do you," Mallory said, his sonorous voice disturbing more bats. They dislodged themselves from the ceiling, to rush past Mallory and Eleanor, toward the chamber they'd exited. They ducked to the filthy floor, more bats in the distance making themselves known with chirps and whistles.

"If it is," Eleanor said, forcing herself to focus on the positives that could be taken from the idea of endless bats, "it means there is an outlet, for what are they eating? This many bats, there will be a food source."

"Mummies, is it?" Mallory said, his mouth quirking.

"Moths," Eleanor insisted, trying to stop her skin from crawling. Few things unsettled her, but bats were near the top of the list. They were literally flighty, easily disturbed, and in the narrow confines of a tomb, they could rush over she and Mallory with ease. Bats weren't fatal, she reassured herself, but even so. If the bats were eating the mummies— "*Moths.*"

"Miss Folley, do bats bother y—"

But before Mallory could finish, another rush of the winged beasts exploded through the corridor. Eleanor crouched, covering her head as the bats wheeled overhead, a small, angry, confined storm. She pictured them filling the chamber, wheeling up the shaft, and spewing out into the night sky from somewhere high above. But worse, she pictured what could be making them flee—what in the tomb was driving them to rush up the corridor and out.

The corridor emptied and quieted and Eleanor peered at Mallory, whose suit was splattered with guano. He looked at her from between his fingers, his expression a mixture of horror and awe. Eleanor's nose wrinkled, the stench in the corridor having become hideous.

"Oh." Mallory straightened and made to brush his lapel clean, but hesitated, as if realizing it would only make the situation worse. "I see now your concern. Or rather—smell your concern."

Eleanor tried not to laugh, because she was likewise splattered, but she failed in this, a low chuckle accompanying them as they continued down the corridor, now also streaked with fresh guano. She could not say how long they walked, the corridor heading straight for what felt like days. Eleanor became aware of how tired her feet were, but also how the guano had come to dry on her clothing, how it flaked from her cheeks and hair. She lifted her hand to brush her fingers clean and realized she could not see the tomb wall—that in fact, the wall had vanished entirely. This caused her to stop walking and Mallory turned to look at her, his mouth gaping open when he turned.

"Wh—"

It was not a tomb corridor they found themselves in, but rather a forest, draped in a warm, clear night. A corridor of trees spread against a flawless starry sky, their crooked trunks making strange, flat shadows upon a wet ground. There was no moon to throw such shadows, but they existed nonetheless. The air had lost its guano tang, and smelled as though it had rained. The closer Eleanor looked, she saw droplets of water on the leaves, like clear pearls. A lumbering creature that appeared pieced together from giraffe and hippo both, a long neck upon a squat body, wandered up to wrap its tongue around a bundle of wet leaves. It stripped the branch with a happy smacking sound. Eleanor did not move, but a guano-drenched woman was of no apparent interest to the beast. It wandered onward into the trees, eating as it went.

"All right," Mallory said. "We were inside the tomb and now we are— Not." Mallory stretched a hand up, as if feeling for the ceiling he would have been able to touch within the tomb's corridor. His hand pressed against a rain-damp branch. "Did you put on any rings?"

Eleanor was reassured by her own smile. "No rings," she said, her voice carrying in the night. She turned in a slow circle, seeing then the pattern of trees. "Look, Virgil. The trees make a corridor all their own."

The trees stretched before and behind, but did not spread outward from the point Eleanor and Mallory occupied. Mallory took Eleanor by the hand, and pulled her in the direction they'd been heading. Their shadows fell before them, though there was no moon at their backs. No moon, and no bats, until Eleanor saw the bats in the trees, hanging as if in sleep. But when she looked closer, she saw they were only the shadows of bats. She could not touch them—her hand passed straight through.

"Is this..." Mallory trailed off, his hand tightening around Eleanor's. "What would it be? The Egyptian underworld? Do they have such a thing—ferrymen waiting at the river, as in Greece? Do we have coins?"

"Maybe Charon will take your nutmegs as payment. But for Egyptians, Duat is the land of the dead," Eleanor answered, beginning to calm as Mallory made her ponder precisely where they found themselves. "Ra travels it every night, poling his boat down a river as he guides the sun into new, glorious life. Tombs are said to connect to that world, but this... I suppose I've never thought about what it would look like, because surely it wasn't an actual place—but rather mythical." Eleanor trailed off. Of course, meeting Anubis in the flesh had challenged her view of what was real and what was not. "Look at this."

In the strange moonlight, she had presumed the tree trunks to be made of bark as any tree would be, but the trunks were comprised of rough chunks of turquoise and lapis, rivers of gold spilling between the stones. It was exquisite work, careful and costly. Beyond the corridor of trees, if Eleanor concentrated, she could see in the distance a rough line of mountains, but the mountains were not stone—they wavered with heat and fire, flames licking the vaulted sky.

"Sycamores of turquoise?" she whispered. She walked around one tree, pulling Mallory after her; she was disconcerted by the way the tree's branches looked, in many cases, like arms, and how some of the branches were swollen, like milk-full breasts. Trees had been said to nourish the dead, Eleanor knew; to see the dead to the end of their journey toward their new life.

"If this is Duat, did we die?" Mallory asked, still holding Eleanor by one hand as if he feared she would vanish; given their prior adventures, she could not fault him. He thumped his free hand against the stone trunk, pushing, but the tree did not budge, seeming as anchored as any tree in the world.

Eleanor peered up at him. "Death by bat guano?" she asked, but knew Mallory had a point. If this was Duat, perhaps it would hold to the rules of the ancient world. If Anubis was real, of course Duat was real. "I don't think we're dead, but if this is Duat, there will be a series of obstacles to overcome, at the end of which stands Anubis to judge us. Though we've already been through his judgment." She shuddered, remembering how Anubis had turned bodies to dust upon finding them unworthy.

They continued along the path made by the trees, but the deeper they walked into the strange land, the more Eleanor became aware of being watched. Stalked was perhaps a better word, for her spine prickled. The night seemed to whisper around them, and it was not the return of bats, but the movement of something they could not see.

"Folley."

Mallory squeezed her hand then released her, moving down the path in longer strides. Something darkened the sand ahead, something that sent Mallory to his knees, staring in disbelief. Eleanor ran to join him, having no idea what he had found, but when she found herself looking at their teacups—the teacups and saucers that had plummeted from the rail of the airship—she laughed.

"No. They can't be."

She crouched beside Mallory, who reached for one cup, but Eleanor grabbed his hand before he could touch it. The china had not so much as cracked, cups and saucers posed as if she and Mallory had only been drinking from them. But the most curious thing was the way the tea itself had marked the sand, and the pattern in which it had spilled.

"It's an ankh," she whispered.

The tea had fallen in the ankh's distinctive teardrop shape, a long tail extending from it, pointing away from her and Mallory, pointing farther down the shadowed path of trees. The shadow of their joined hands made the crossbar of the ankh, completing the strange image. It was male and female both, liquid and solid, and it was, Eleanor thought, a key. An ankh pressed to a mouth bestowed life, breath, being.

The key her father had sought? But how did one pick up an ankh that had been made of spilled tea and shadows?

"We work together," Mallory said as if knowing where her thoughts had gone. "Just as this tomb has asked us every step of the way so far. Partners. Two hands. Don't break the shadow—free hands, Folley."

Mallory slid his free hand into the sand and Eleanor followed suit. She expected to feel only wet sand, and while she could smell the tea he had brewed—bergamot and black leaves—what she felt beneath her fingers was startling. Buried in the sand was an ankh, revealing itself to be carved from black soapstone as she and Mallory drew it into the strange moonlight. It was like nothing Eleanor had seen in her travels, unmarked by any words. Only the marks of the tools used to carve it remained, the black stone splattered with white in its hollows and curves. It was warm to the touch, as if it had been resting within an oven, or a cup of tea.

Once the ankh was freed of the sand, they felt able to break the shadow their hands had made over the surface of the object. The ankh did not dissolve into tea or sand, but rested heavily in Eleanor's hand as Mallory drew back. She closed her hand around it, worrying that the world might vanish around her as it had when she'd slipped Anubis's rings onto her fingers. But the world stayed solid and Mallory's grin made her smile in return.

It was the teacups that fell to pieces once the ankh was withdrawn, the china glittering in the strange light that fell through the branches of the trees. The cups cracked into dust, becoming one with the sand to fill the hollowed space the ankh once had.

IV.

Eleanor and Mallory continued to follow the sandy path between the turquoise and gold trees. The world beyond the trees made no sense to Eleanor, for it did not seem to be wholly Duat. From time to time, she thought she glimpsed the tomb walls. Were they still within its underground confines? And if *that* were so, what then was the sky wheeling overhead? It was so bright, so full of stars that looked like a river of spilled milk, she could not quite believe it had been manufactured for them. To what end? Mallory had no guesses.

Also in the "high probability of not manufactured" category, Eleanor placed the creatures that stalked them from beyond the tree's sheltered path. Each possessed a human-shaped body—much as Egyptian gods did—but their heads were grotesque, one comprised of what appeared to be gushing blood. It was impossible to say where the blood began, or how it continued to circulate without the benefit of veins, arteries, or in fact, skin. Another resembled a scimitar-mouthed beetle, nothing so delicate as a scarab for the blades which swept outward from its mouth were curved and ragged, hanging with the tattered flesh of someone who'd gotten too close. A solitary beast followed these others, scooping their excrement from the sand, shoveling it into its black maw.

The trees appeared to be a specific line of demarcation, dividing one region from another. Eleanor had tried again to step between the trees, to wander from the path, and while she could, the beasts had made a quick, riotous approach. Unlike her, they seemed to know the trees for the boundary they were, for they did not attempt to push their way through the stone trunks, allowing her to return to the path. Would harm come to them if they tried, or if the trees would simply not allow them to pass? She felt as though they were being herded toward a destination, but after what seemed hours of walking, she and Mallory had not found an end to the path or trees. The strange moonless moonlight had not changed, eased, or given way to a sunlit day.

"Aside from our companions, this grows tedious," Mallory said, stopping in the middle of the path.

Eleanor stopped and looked at him, watching over his shoulder as the beasts beyond the tree line crept closer. They looked like shadows until she tried to discern more features; then, they came into hideous focus. From her jacket pocket, she withdrew her father's journal, spreading the pages open to read from the start.

"I don't think my father got very far," she said. "His notes are mostly speculation—perhaps research he did, see here this: imiut." Her finger traced over the word, hastily scrawled in lowercase letters. But it had been underlined twice, causing the word to stand out from any others upon the page.

"A clue?" Mallory asked. He leaned in to look at the page, at the word.

"I wouldn't think so—an imiut fetish is part of funeral rites, however given where we find ourselves..." She lifted her head from the writing, to look at the strange world beyond the trees. "Maybe he knew the tomb was a door to the underworld? A door, given he was searching for a key, which he could not find, given he was working alone."

"And why alone?" Mallory asked. "He and your mother worked in the field together, did they not?"

Eleanor's breath hitched. "Until she left." She flipped to the front of the journal, looking for a date, but there was none to be found; her father, immaculate record keeper, had made no record of when he had begun the journal. Speculation settled like a stone in her belly. "All right. If my father were researching this tomb after her disappearance, he was also emphatic during this time that she was dead, not that she had willingly left her family to live in the ancient world."

Mallory gently plucked the journal from Eleanor's hold, thumbing through the pages. "Your father knew from the start, what your mother intended." Mallory ran a finger over the name "Hatshepsut" within the journal. "And knew that this tomb was believed to be that of Hatshepsut. There is no question the rings had been connected to the pharaoh in your parents' research—your mother knew where she was going, because of her own mother. Do you suppose..."

When he trailed off, Eleanor took a breath. "Go on."

"Your father didn't have the rings, nor your ability to travel with them," Mallory said. He closed the journal and eyed Eleanor. "We have plainly passed into Someplace Else. Maybe your father thought this was a route to your mother—not that it was her tomb, or her resting place, for he knew she was alive elsewhere. But maybe he believed this was a way to reach her even after she had gone."

Eleanor shook her head, a low wind finally stirring the air around them. It smelled foul, worse than the bats, and outside the treeline, the creatures paced a restless line, snarling and slobbering, the one still shoving its mouth full of refuse the others dropped.

"To what end, Virgil?" she whispered.

Mallory closed the brief distance between them, sliding the journal back into Eleanor's jacket pocket. From there, his arm encircled her, to pull her close against him. "I have not known you long and yet I would miss you, Eleanor, if you went. Your father built a life with this woman, had a child with her. Though he knew what she planned, isn't it possible he wished to see her again? That even if angry with her, he wanted to see her one more time? Convince her to—" But here Mallory trailed off.

"To come home?" Eleanor asked. She slid her arms around Mallory, inside his jacket where he was warmest and smelled less like bat guano. "I don't think he could have convinced her of anything, but maybe he wanted to. It's hard to say—given that all I believed of him turned out to be a lie."

Mallory pressed his mouth against the top of Eleanor's head, a slow, warm kiss. "Not everything. He's always loved you, and it could not have been easy to see the pain his only child was in, after Dalila left. She didn't leave only him, remember. She left a daughter—and from all accounts, you were none to easy to live with afterward."

"I was not," Eleanor allowed, smiling up at Mallory.

47

Hand in hand, they walked on in companionable silence for a long while. The time remained hard for Eleanor to gauge, for the light of the world never changed. She did not hunger or thirst, and this bothered her, for if time were passing, her body should know it and register it. It must have also bothered Mallory, for he reminded her to drink and often as they continued to walk the path of trees.

As they walked, a creeping uncertainty began to overtake Eleanor; she felt as though something were on her very heels, though a glance behind proved them as alone as ever. Still, she grew cold and at her side, Mallory seemed only a shadow; a shadow that was more wolf than man, hunched and bristled in the strange moonlight. She felt queasy and he smelled like a grave too long open.

"Mallory," she ventured. "You said you've never sought another of your kind. Of our kind." Eleanor lifted Mallory's hand, to study the band of silver around his index finger. Amid the carefully fashioned skulls were the words *Viver disce, cognita mori*. It was more than a simple memento mori; it was a focus for Mallory, to help him come back from his wolf form if ever he were stuck.

"Mmm." Mallory nodded. "In my work, I've always been mindful—always looking for someone who might share my...unusual qualities." His hand tightened in Eleanor's. "But I never crossed paths with someone like that, until you, Miss Folley." In the eternal twilight, his smile was swift as quicksilver. "Not a single one."

"What are the odds of that?" Eleanor asked in a near

whisper, talking more to herself than him. The cold shadow spilled over her shoulders now, wreathing her neck. "In all those years...every place you have been..." She stole a look at him, but suddenly could not stand the shadow of the wolf beneath his skin. "And why— Why me?"

"Eleanor."

She was shaking now, dread flooding her. It was as though she stood in the Nile, the black river swelling against her belly, against her breasts and throat. She could feel the black water growing higher, though it was sand upon which she stood. She ached to pull her hand from Mallory's, even as his grip upon her tightened. She told herself she tried to pull her hand free, even as she was standing absolutely still.

"Let me go," she whispered, but even as she watched Mallory's hand open, she could not move her own. The black water licked higher.

"Eleanor. Tell me what troubles you."

Mallory's hand closed around hers again and he drew her to sitting, holding her as she shook. Eleanor felt as cold as winter, but still being pulled down into black waters. Waters so deep she could see nothing of herself once they swallowed her.

"Why me?" she whispered again.

She *knew* it was irrational—beyond the shadow of the wolf within Mallory, she saw the arc of the trees above them, their leaves wet with rain, yet not dripping. She remembered where they were—some version of Duat where monsters beyond the living world stalked and slavered after them; she remembered the ankh and the gift of the tomb, that Mallory had wanted her to see this place—

What had he known? Was this part of his vile plan? To bring her here? To bury her in this strange world so that he could continue being the only one of his kind in the world above?

A hollow laugh escaped Eleanor and the world swam out of focus until Mallory's warm hands pressed against her cheeks. He took gentle hold of her face, whispering words she could not hear. Not until she allowed herself to focus on the gold within the brown of Mallory's eyes; he took comfort in this as she always had—a hint of the beast he always kept so well controlled. He meant nothing by bringing her here—had no desire to be one of a kind. Eleanor knew these things, yet the idea that he did wish to be alone still draped her, like a cape.

"Mal—" She couldn't get his name out. "Only because—"

"Why you," he was whispering. "A thousand reasons why you. *Mon Dieu*, you're growing cold, Eleanor—that's not one of them. Come on. Don't— What—"

Mallory's hands slipped from her cheeks, to her shoulders where the shadow lay heavily. Eleanor felt his fingers hook into it, as if it were an article of clothing, and her breath hitched. When Mallory's hold eased, the dread returned. It coiled around her throat as might a living hand.

"Get. It. Off," she rasped.

Eleanor twisted, as if to shake the shadow loose, but it did not come free. Two, she thought; partners. One alone would be consumed within the tomb's horrors, but two might survive. Two together. She closed her hand into the sand path, lifting her eyes to look beyond the stone-crusted trees, where a beast crouched. Eleanor saw then how its horrible shadow stretched between the gem trees, how it had made itself thin to reach her, and how it clawed up her legs, around her belly, over her shoulders. When Eleanor met its green, venomous gaze, the beast pulled, shadow as claws, hauling her out of Mallory's arms.

Eleanor dug her hands into the sand, but the grains began to spiral away from her, as they had in the first tomb chamber they'd encountered. Eleanor could not hold to it, so lunged for Mallory. Mallory was in motion, dropping his pack to the ground, so Eleanor wrapped herself around what she could, the strong length of his leg. Mallory pulled the folded shovel from his pack, snapping it into a straight rod of metal in one hard motion. With the blade of the shovel, Mallory stabbed through the shadow where it draped the sand.

Outside the trees, the beast howled. It was the sound of a living body being turned inside out, and Eleanor thought she might drown in it. The black water once licking her had grown warm, the temperature of blood, as the keening cry continued. Mallory's strikes against the shadow became more certain, even as Eleanor felt her human form slipping away. She cried out in panic, for if she lost the use of her arms, she would lose her hold on Mallory, and be pulled away. She would be melted down, made small enough to slip as shadows did through the trunks, until she was in the maw of the beast.

Anger and fear clawed up her legs, up her shoulders, until she screamed. Cold smoke seeping from a frozen throat—it swallowed Eleanor bit by bit.

The shadow was thick, not unlike a blanket, but Mallory made good use of the shovel, burying its pointed tip into the shadow to at last sever it from the beast beyond the trees. The length of shadow whipped toward the creature, withdrawing from the trees, while the shadow that still cloaked Eleanor shredded. It felt like cloud of grasshoppers flying in panic, so it was Mallory's hands Eleanor focused on; she mimicked his motions, brushing the shadow off and away, until it fell as burning embers to the sandy path. Within the sheltering bower of the trees, the shadow perished, its creature shrieking as it fled into the desert beyond. Its shadow trailed behind it, wet upon the sand as if trailing blood.

"Eleanor."

Mallory flung the shovel away, but when he might have gathered Eleanor into his arms, he hesitated. She remembered with perfect clarity what she had thought—his vile plans for bringing her here, and why he courted her at all; remembered too how she'd thought she could not move inside his hold. Disgust rolled through her, even as she knew it had been the creature, its shadow cultivating these horrors inside her mind. Mallory, she knew, treasured everything about her and would never hold her back—not when he could run alongside her.

Eleanor reached for Mallory, pulling herself back into his arms. When his own locked around her, Eleanor allowed herself to breathe, closing her eyes to the strangeness of the world around them. In the circle of his arms, where life seemed most warm, Eleanor calmed. He no longer smelled of death, but of himself—as she was sure he always had. She looked beyond the trees and could see no sign of the foul creature, only the ragged path of its spilling blood, before another beast scooped the soiled sand into its mouth.

"Forgive me, Virgil. That...was not me."

Mallory pulled back only enough to cup Eleanor's face, dropping a kiss against her forehead. "*Tesorina*, there is nothing to forgive." He rubbed his cheek against hers, then looked her straight in the eye. "There are a thousand reasons why you," he said as he had said before, and before she could protest, "and it would be a lie to deny your ability to change forms was not among of them. But it's like a book, aye? And you open it—I open *you*—and discover you are a doorway, which takes me into the stars where I finally learn to breathe, and then I'm falling—falling all over again."

Mallory's mouth was warm when Eleanor kissed him, heedless of where they were, for she felt that sometimes the clock must be stopped, no matter the circumstances, and she knew no better way than this. The world retreated when she fitted her mouth against Mallory's, when she straddled him as no proper lady should, in her trousers and jacket, and threaded her fingers into his riotous hair. When he met her with the same fervor and need, only then did the world right itself and when she opened her eyes, it was to the brightening colors of dawn against the very distant horizon.

"Can you see that?" she murmured. Maybe it was her

alone, but Mallory nodded.

Beyond the mountains of fire, and the rivers of liquid gold, the horizon grew slowly warm and bright, as if the sky were sucking the rivers dry. Eleanor leaned into Mallory, taking another kiss before she even considered letting him go, letting him up. As much as the creature had made her doubt, she reveled in the certainly of what she knew here and now. She plucked the shovel from the sand, the last of the shadow sliding from its tip like ash.

Mallory retrieved his pack, and checked Eleanor's, offering her a canteen. Eleanor traded it for the shovel, taking a long drink of the water that was beginning to taste like metal. Her gaze strayed down the path of trees, which to her surprise, was much shorter than she remembered. She could see its end, a door set into the ground, scattered with sand. But she could also see a pair of eyes shining in the rising sun. The squat body of *something* sat near the door and Eleanor stared.

"Something is down there, Virgil," she said softly and he turned to look.

"A shadow something?" He raised the shovel in anticipation.

To Eleanor, it didn't look much worse than what they had faced—certainly no larger, though size was rarely an indication of viciousness. Some of the worst things in the world were tiny, some of the most gentle the largest. With their gear gathered, they walked toward the door and its attendant. Eleanor shuddered at the way the brightening light cast shadows; they were not natural, stretching toward the rising light, rather than away. Eleanor didn't want to touch a single one of them, but the tree shadows she had to cross proved harmless, ordinary, and by the time they reached they door, she'd stopped wanting to jump at every single darkness.

The creature beside the door was part flesh, part metal, and Eleanor could not put a name to it until it moved from the crouch it had assumed. It rose on four cog and wire legs, to stretch in the rising light like a cat. Its long articulated tail flicked behind while its very-human face, delicate in its angles but neither male nor female, regarded them with something akin to boredom. Its lips were painted black, a gold ankh painted in their exact center appearing to seal them shut. The sides of its lion's body heaved with a deep breath, a golden metallic heart set within its chest. Eleanor could see every gear, cogs turning with every beat, but could also see the muscle that ran below; muscle and blood both, fused into a clockwork chamber that glowed with bright, blue gaslight.

"Sphinx!" Mallory whispered in surprise.

"I have a name, human," the sphinx said.

"Is that your riddle, then?" Mallory asked. He lowered the shovel and crouched to sphinx-level, studying the creature.

"You aren't in Greece," the sphinx said, settling back on its golden haunches. Its hazel eyes narrowed and Eleanor was surprised it didn't fall asleep as it regarded them. She crouched beside Mallory, captivated.

"Only Greek sphinxes bestow riddles?" Eleanor asked. The eyes flicked open, framed by long lashes and perfectly black kohl. Eleanor marveled at that, but noted that one of the sphinx's feet had disturbingly human fingers instead of the metallic fingers the other possessed. This, too, was a riddle, Eleanor felt certain.

"Oh I've riddles if you want them, but who has time for Greek nonsense?" The sphinx blinked at Eleanor, then Mallory, before its fanged mouth opened in a protracted yawn. "I am Mugabalah, and you, having come this far, presume to enter the door." At that, the sphinx tapped the wood door with a metal foot. The wood door rang hollow, a soft cloud of dust rising as if to prove that none had come this way in a long while. The door was nearly black, its surface covered in scratches and pockmarks,

"No riddle? Then there's no cost to enter?" Mallory asked. He folded the shovel and tucked it into his pack, the sphinx watching him all the while. Mallory glanced at Eleanor who thought it unlikely as well; there was always a cost, especially on this journey.

Mugabalah's ears twitched in its mane of black hair. "There is a cost," the sphinx said, "but none that this tomb's maker established. To be certain, this is *my* cost, mortals. If you will not pay, you shall not pass, though that would be dreadfully boring, wouldn't it?" The sphinx stretched again, metal and flesh fingers digging into the sand. "You've beaten the shadow thing, after all."

At that, Eleanor looked behind them, startled to see that the path they had followed was gone. The sanctuary provided by the trees had also vanished as if they had never been. Empty desert stretched as far as she could see; no rivers to carry Ra, no mountains made of fire. But the horrid creatures that had stalked them, she could feel those like a lingering blight, and she whined, alarmed by how quick the jackal within her rose in an effort to flee. If they remained within the tomb, its walls were still not visible.

"Speak your cost, sphinx," Eleanor said. "We would pass, for there is no way back."

Mugabalah smiled, its face grown as mysterious as any who kept a secret they must also soon divulge. The sphinx came to look uncomfortable, glancing over its shoulder at the desert waste that stretched beyond.

"Too long have I waited," Mugabalah whispered, "too long have I sat. Too long at my duty, while Anubis grows fat."

Eleanor's skin prickled at the mention of Anubis. She exchanged a glance with Mallory—if this were not a riddle, because riddles were Greek nonsense, they waited for the sphinx to speak again. When it did not, Eleanor felt a little panic clawing inside her. The jackal inside her wanted out, specifically so that it might chase this infuriating creature to exhaustion.

"Sphinx—"

"Too long have I waited," Mugabalah repeated, its head swinging back to Eleanor and Mallory, "too long have I sat." Something akin to a purr emerged from the beast and it lunged for Eleanor. She yelped, but there was no attack, the creature rubbing its cheek against Eleanor's thigh, the way a cat would to mark its territory. "Too long!"

"You—" Eleanor eyed Mallory over the purring sphinx

and realized then what it meant. "You want to go with us."

The sphinx put a shoulder to the sand, rolling as a cat to expose its lion's belly. Eleanor wanted very much to pet the belly, but resisted, knowing full well it was the perfect way to lose a hand. She looked instead at the old door, at the depression in the sand beside it. The scratches upon the wood could have easily been made by the sphinx itself as it sat there, not by those who had otherwise tried to enter. If there had been no riddle, surely the door opened on its own? There was a knob in its center, but no lock to bar the way.

"Mallory," Eleanor said exactly as he said "Folley." Eleanor raised an eyebrow, waiting.

"Maybe the lack of a riddle is the riddle," he said, and rose from the sand in which they crouched. He went to the door and the sphinx made no move to challenge him, only watched with Eleanor as Mallory tried to turn the knob. It did not move, which didn't seem to surprise him, or Eleanor. "If the rule of two holds here, too, Mugabalah could not pass alone."

Eleanor joined Mallory at the door, the sphinx coming to its feet to sit and watch. With Eleanor's hands upon his, the knob turned easily, the sandy door falling inward to reveal a staircase of stone twisting down into the ceaseless dark. The air that came up was cold, as if they weren't in a desert at all.

"At last," the sphinx said.

"But what's down there?" Eleanor asked. "And why do you need it?"

As Eleanor asked, Mugabalah padded past her, onto the first steps that led ever down. "There's a tomb down there, don't you know? Or did you wander in unthinkingly?" The sphinx raised an eyebrow much as Eleanor had, then padded down the stairs, its metal tail flicking the air as it went.

Eleanor and Mallory wasted no time in lighting the lantern and following the sphinx as it went. The steps were slippery with sand and dust and Eleanor kept a hand upon the wall as she walked farther down. She waited when Mallory paused to push the door shut; he didn't want to chance anything following them down and Eleanor was only in agreement.

Why a sphinx needed a tomb, Eleanor didn't know, but neither did she dwell on the question, focusing instead on the steps. They spiraled down in a perfect circle, the air growing colder and more damp with every turn. The steps had been cut from the very limestone they butted up against, the walls strangely smooth though here and there, Eleanor felt a hiccup in the stone. She wished for wall sconces, for something to keep the way lit, for no matter how far they walked, their pocket of light never expanded. It was as if they were encased in a golden bubble, falling through the dark. Mallory stayed close and the sphinx never quite left the reach of the lantern light; the tip of its tail bounced ahead of Eleanor, circling down and down. The light within the beast's chest did little to illuminate the way, ghosting over walls and steps briefly before the sphinx turned another revolution.

Farther down, they slowed, the steps choked with debris. They had to clear steps with hammers and shovels, and Eleanor felt the change in the stone; it broke in sheets, which limestone never would and was smoother beneath Eleanor's fingers. She could not see the color of the walls to properly judge, so plucked a tiny piece of it from the rubble and bit into it, confirming it was shale by the way it crumpled, by the way clay and silt raked up against her teeth. A less stable building material to be sure, but the tomb builder wouldn't have exactly been able to reroute the tunnels at this stage of the work.

"Be careful, Mallory," Eleanor said. "The rock is less stable here."

"I'll have a care too, then," Mugabalah said with a soft hiss as they came to the end of the staircase.

The corridor led in one direction, the sphinx heading that way without pause. Eleanor examined the walls that now blocked them in. They appeared much like the first walls of the tomb they'd seen, carved with vague warnings and dire predictions. Eleanor glanced at Mallory in the lantern light.

"A little more than you bargained for?" she asked.

Mallory's laugh echoed in the corridor. "I'll say. If this isn't the best gift you've ever received, Miss Folley, I will eat my hat."

Eleanor fell into step alongside Mallory as they continued down the corridor, the sphinx's footsteps making a clear path for them to follow in the scattered sand. "You don't have a hat, Mallory," Eleanor said softly, "only three small nutmegs."

Mallory's hand closed around her own and Eleanor allowed herself a smile as they walked on. Exhaustion was beginning to make the world fuzzy; she longed for a blanket and a pillow and hours in which to explore them. Was she growing soft? She had spent more than her share of nights in tombs, in the desert, in caves, and swamps. Given what she had encountered in her explorations, this tomb was proving gentle, even with the horrors they had seen in Duat.

Here, there were no horrors, only an endless corridor. The sphinx had decided to sit, having wandered far ahead; when Eleanor and Mallory caught up with it, it flicked its tail.

"Too long have I sat," Mugabalah whispered.

"We could have left you at the door," Eleanor said. "If this tomb requires us to move in pairs, you're a third wheel, sphinx."

Eleanor did not expect the sphinx to be alarmed, but the expression that came to rest upon the beast's unsettling face could be nothing else. Eleanor felt strangely sympathetic toward it. How long had it waited outside that door before being let in? When she asked, the sphinx gave her no answer, shaking its head. Sand whispered out of its mane, the lantern light reflecting in unshed tears.

"I cannot say," it said.

It was then Eleanor dared touch the sphinx, resting her hand atop the magnificent mane, before dragging her fingers through. The hair was thick and coarse, but warm—alive. The sphinx exhaled a purr and butted its head into Eleanor's hand.

"See there!" Mugabalah exclaimed and, like a cat, bolted into the dark corridor.

"What is there to see?" she asked, and he raised the lantern as they walked on.

The corridor curved slightly, but from there, its end could

be seen. A doorway that Eleanor was certain had once been square was beginning to collapse, the shale starting to give way after thousands of years. Like the other doors, this was lined with warnings, but the sphinx paid them no heed. The sphinx did not so much as pause before it bounded into the darkness beyond the buckled opening.

"Sphinx!" Mallory called after it, but the beast did not return.

It was then the floor made a familiar motion, one that sent Eleanor and Mallory sliding. Eleanor could not quite believe the shale had chosen *that* exact moment to buckle—was something mechanical was working unseen, heaving the floor beneath them, tipping them into the maw that the door seemed to form itself into?

And how much further could they possibly fall? Eleanor's fingers slipped from the door's crumbling edge, nails cracking painfully against the limestone. When did one simply fall though the other side of the world and into the stars beyond? Beneath them, Eleanor saw water—water! A river at the bottom of the world.

V.

The river was not salty, nor was it sweet; it was the foulest thing Eleanor had ever tasted—even allowing that she had sampled Auberon's cooked eels. The water was thick as sludge against her tongue and though Eleanor was aware she was not breathing—aware too of the hard smack and plunge of Mallory behind her as his body struck hers—she was desperate to get the water out of her mouth. To have it stop touching her. Breath seemed the least of her worries as the water slithered over her. Into her.

The river moved in a way that water should not move—a knowing way that reacted to her own flailing. Still, Eleanor bucked in an effort to escape its hold. She felt Mallory scrambled to do the same, but the water clung everywhere, and seeming possessed of hands—of claws—pulled them ever deeper into its black mouth.

One hand grasped the slimy shore, but she couldn't pull herself out; the water wrapped around her tight. Then, the firmness of Mallory's shoulder lodged against her backside. He thrust her forward, and she curled a hand into his sodden hair—if she was going out, he was coming with her. Together, they flopped on the sandy shore, spluttering.

The sphinx had survived the fall as well, and took to stripping sodden packs from Eleanor and Mallory alike. It occurred to Eleanor to protest, but the notion that the sphinx might run off with their gear made her laugh.

"Now who becomes the third wheel?" Mugabalah asked

as it worked.

Eleanor closed her eyes, trying to breathe evenly. "History was right about your lot," she whispered, feeling Mallory's hand tighten around hers. She felt, too, his laughter as it rumbled through him.

Slowly, Eleanor sat up, discovering the lantern had not survived this fall. It scattered in gleaming pieces across the riverbank, faint blue light playing over the glass. It was the sphinx's gaslight alone that allowed them to see, even though the shell of light was thinner than that of the lantern. The wavering blue light did not give away much about their location—the river twisted into the darkness in both directions, a great and seemingly empty darkness yawning above.

Out of the river's hold, the water was merely water; it dripped from their clothing and hair normally, darkening the sand and stone. The cold had gone, however, the familiar warmth of the tomb beginning to dry Eleanor's clothes. She helped Mallory up from the sand and watched the sphinx prowl away.

"Mugabalah!" Mallory called after the sphinx, but it paid no attention, padding into the dark.

Instantly, the darkness closed around Eleanor and Mallory. Eleanor raked her hands through her hair, before knotting it back into its usual chignon.

"All right," she murmured. "We've still flint and steel? When anything dries…we can burn it? Can wolves see in the dark, Mallory? Can jackals?" She tilted her head. Did their animal forms give them what the situation called for? She had no desire to carry her pack on her jackal back. Jackals didn't tote supplies with them!

"I see very well in the dark," Mallory said, and while Eleanor thought he referred to his wolf form, his hand slid unerringly around her waist, to pull her close. "As man or wolf."

At this, his mouth covered Eleanor's without err and she pushed their circumstances aside, to enjoy the feel of Mallory's mouth. The idea that he could see well in all this darkness was somehow exciting—they weren't at a dead end? Mallory was as wet as she, but was warmer and she slid her hands into his jacket, around his waist, as if she could burrow into him. It was then the shriek echoed through the cavern. Eleanor pulled out of the kiss, but Mallory held her as the shriek deepened. It was inhuman, followed by the sound of leathery wings flapping against close walls.

In the distant darkness, the sphinx's blue light appeared, growing closer and closer. Eleanor bent to retrieve the revolver in her sodden pack—it was perhaps water-logged and useless, but its weight in her hand made her feel better. Until cold water dribbled from the chamber and down her wrist. If the sphinx was leading something— If something was following—

The sphinx leapt for she and Mallory, cowering behind them as above something massive and black swooped past. Eleanor could see nothing, but the air rushed over them, fetid and rank, and the creature's wings dipped low enough to brush her and Mallory's heads, before it lifted higher.

"Hellfire," Mallory whispered. He turned, putting Eleanor against his back and she could feel his heart racing through the leather coat that still wrapped him. The sphinx twined against and into their legs, an overgrown, terrified cat.

"Mugabalah, what was it?" Eleanor whispered, listening for, but not hearing, those massive wings overhead. Still, keeping an arm on Mallory, she crouched down to look the sphinx in the eyes. The sphinx's face had gone pale, the kohl around its eyes not having smudged despite the tears that streamed.

"Harpy," the sphinx murmured, butting its head into Eleanor's shoulder.

Eleanor looked up, but saw no sign of it circling back. But it was so dark, Eleanor doubted she would. "Aren't harpies also Greek nonsense?" Eleanor asked, gently rubbing the sphinx's closest ear through its beautiful mane. The sphinx shuddered and sat hard on its haunches.

"Greeks brought plenty of nonsense with them, didn't they?"

The darkness beyond the glow of the sphinx light remained quiet and eventually the trio broke from their huddle. Eleanor could not shake the idea that they would see more strangeness before they had finished with the tomb's mysteries. The sphinx paced downriver, seeming certain it was the proper direction for them to travel.

"There was nothing upriver," Mugabalah murred as Eleanor and Mallory strapped their damp packs back on.

Eleanor looked that way, as if her eyes might suddenly be able to pierce the dark; it remained as stubborn as ever and she looked back to the sphinx, who had taken to nibbling the sand from between its toes.

"What is it you seek, sphinx?" she asked. "What is down here, beyond a tomb?"

"And do you know where it rests?" Mallory added. He stood beside Eleanor and sucked water from their dwindling canteens.

"The tomb you seek," Mugabalah said, "was not made for the meek." The sphinx appraised Eleanor and Mallory with a haughty look, eyes narrowed again. "Given what has transpired, I predict it will not devour you—you two come paired as was written." With that, the sphinx padded off, downriver this time.

Eleanor and Mallory fell into step behind the sphinx, the gaslight in its chest serving as a torch of sorts—dim though it was, it allowed them to see the rough cut river to their left. At their right hand spread only darkness, until the darkness was eclipsed by the return of the tomb walls. Eleanor could not say when it happened; one minute it wasn't there and the next it was. She placed her hand flat against it, watching as Mallory did the same. The river fell behind them, tomb walls stretching into the distance.

The corridors were still of shale, the walls showing signs of stress the deeper they walked. The walls were not marked here, but smooth save for the cracks that had begun to split them. Debris cluttered the narrow hall, until they turned a corner and the corridor widened. It was not a full-sized chamber they found themselves in, but neither was it only a corridor between chambers. Six columns held the ceiling firm, their bulbous widths still resplendent with paints that sough to turn them into flower stems; against the ceiling, flowers bloomed in a blue and gold starscape. None of the walls showed signs of stress, the columns keeping the room intact.

"Mallory, look at this." Eleanor turned in a slow circle, admiring the room.

"The mother kept gardens fair," Mugabalah said as it paced into the colonnade, "as if anyone would dare—make the desert bloom."

"The mother?" Mallory whispered.

Eleanor was thankful for the way Mallory's warm hand closed around hers. If this tomb did have a connection to her mother, there was no one else she wanted at her side. The idea of gardens called to mind Hatshepsut's temple, the myrrh, and the pools of water. The way the trees had parted to reveal Eleanor's mother, who had stepped back through time to find her own mother serving the ancient pharaoh.

"Lotus and myrrh," the sphinx said, "and water, too. She bathed the desert from her skin with water—can you imagine?"

Mugabalah passed from the room and Eleanor and Mallory followed so as to not be lost in the darkness. Eleanor noted that the walls had begun to change—they were marked with warnings again, but these began to gave way to more traditional hieroglyphs, those speaking about the tomb's occupant. It began with mentions of the Queen of the Mirror—Eleanor's own grandmother, pulled back in time when she had discovered the rings of Anubis. When Eleanor and Mallory paused together, the sphinx turned to them. Blue gaslight flooded over the markings, and Eleanor exhaled, daring herself to touch them. She still expected the stone to give way, for time to pull her away, too, but these things did not happen. Sand gritted under her fingers, but nothing more.

"Sagira el Jabari," Mugabalah said. "Oh—*oh*, you are her blood—Anubis ever nearby." It turned and continued down the corridor.

Eleanor did not move. If Anubis were close, she could not feel him, so reached out with her mind, asking for him. *Anubis?* When there came no answer, she fell into step behind the sphinx.

The corridor had at its end a door, tall and golden, but before that, set into nooks within the corridor walls, stood eleven sphinx. Eleanor and Mallory drew themselves up short at the sight of them, but the sphinx who had traveled with them continued on, stopping at each nook. The sphinx appeared to be sleeping, eyes closed, chests still without even a single breath until Mugabalah pressed a kiss to the lips and woke them.

"Astounding," Mallory said.

As each sphinx woke, they looked upon Mugabalah in astonishment. They were each made as Mugabalah had been made, of flesh and clockwork both, hearts burning in their chests. They stretched and purred and twined around each other in greeting, and Mugabalah frolicked among them until the last was woken. Then, the sphinx padded back to Eleanor and Mallory.

"The way is prepared," Mugabalah said, then sauntered past the pair, down the corridor the way they had come. "We stand to defend."

The sphinx followed, leaving Eleanor and Mallory in an empty and suddenly quiet corridor. The corridor should have been dark without the glowing gaslight of the sphinx, but the doors at the end of the corridor had a glow all their own. Eleanor could not say how, or why it was so, and she did not care. What she cared about lay beyond the doors themselves, but now that it came time to open them and enter, she could not move.

"Have your feet stuck to the floor?" Mallory asked, wrapping an arm around her shoulders from behind.

"Yes," Eleanor said.

"Mine have not. Come on." Mallory moved around her swiftly, taking her by the hand. "We've come all this way, and if you think I'm not going into that room, you don't know me in the least bit. Did you hear what Mugabalah said, it knows of your grandmother? Whatever rests behind these doors is part of what you seek. The whole truth—whatever it may be. Grandmother, mother—putting ghosts to rest, can one do that?"

Eleanor squeezed Mallory's hand. "One cannot, but two can. Help me with this door already." Her voice was light, but forced; Eleanor felt the way she had when Mallory had first contacted her months before, when everything in her life had turned upside down. When everything had fallen beautifully apart.

The door before them was as tall as two men, one standing on the shoulders of another. Much like the trees they had passed through, the door was a work of art, the gold threaded through with what looked like rivers of bright blue faience. There were no knobs, no locks, and when Eleanor and Mallory pressed their hands to the surface, nothing moved. Pushing, sliding, and knocking yielded no results, and they stepped back in confusion, if not dismay.

"The tomb cannot work in a way it has not already, can it?" Mallory asked. "Everything has required two."

"Unless we're...elsewhere," Eleanor murmured. She drew her arms around herself, contemplating the hallway. "If we genuinely passed through Duat...we could be anywhere."

"But we're not," Mallory insisted. "No. This door will hold to the rules. One doesn't build a tomb and then change the rules at the final step." He tried the door on his own and it did not budge. "Maybe the sphinx should have remained— these empty nooks..." He ducked into one, and Eleanor tried not to laugh.

"Mugabalah said the way had been prepared—the sphinx aren't necessary," she said, but considered what the creature might have meant by that. The preparing of a way, the opening of a door into a— "Mallory." Eleanor grinned, and wriggled out of her pack. From its damp interior, she pulled out the ankh she and Mallory had made on the path of trees. "Anubis prepares the way. An ankh is placed against the mouth, giving the breath of life—the way Mugabalah did with those sphinx. The breath of life opens a door, doesn't it?"

"Doors don't have mouths," Mallory said, but walked with Eleanor to the door again.

There was nothing on the surface of the door to indicate a mouth, a place where the ankh might fit, only rivers of faience within smooth gold. "*We* have mouths," Eleanor said, "and I *am* a daughter of Anubis." Holding the ankh in her right hand and placing her left flat against the door, she nodded to Mallory whose eyes simmered gold in the door's light. "Come and take this breath, Virgil."

The soapstone ankh grew heavy in her hand as Mallory pressed his hand to the door and leaned toward the ankh. Eleanor did not let him touch it, however; she made certain that *she* placed its uppermost curve against his lips, so the breath was given and not taken. When nothing happened and Mallory made to step back, Eleanor shook her head.

"Anubis?" she whispered.

The weight of the world pressed down on Eleanor. It seemed she could feel how far they had come, their path like a spiraling golden thread in the dark of her mind. They had come so far, and bypassed dangers untold; she knew they would not fail here, for this was the door and the way. They had made the ankh from their joined hands and she *could* bestow the breath. She could, for the blood of the jackal ran through her as surely as the Nile ran through Egypt. She felt her heartbeat—slow and slower, Anubis's shadow overtaking her as he weighed her heart yet again.

"Anubis." This time, a demand.

Daughter.

Anubis's voice clawed down Eleanor's spine and the tomb air grew cold, the scent of rotting flesh filling the small space. Within her, the weight of Anubis's hand left her heart; he carefully withdrew and allowed her the space, the breath. Before her, Mallory's eyes flared gold as the wolf within him made itself known; Eleanor pictured the beast pacing and snarling as Anubis took his leave.

When a sudden cold wind lifted their skin to gooseflesh and spun in tiny dervishes through their hair, the door moved. Eleanor felt it slide beneath her hand, moving on ancient, hidden mechanisms, until the chamber beyond beckoned them, black and eternal. The air that rushed out was clotted with rot and dust, the exhalation of a thousand dead bodies even if only one now resided within.

Mallory's eyes went wide with surprise and he laughed, keeping his hand on the door as it continued to move aside. Eleanor lowered the ankh from Mallory's mouth slowly, uncertain if the door would stop when the stone left his lips. When the door did not stop, she exhaled the breath she'd been holding, the door notching itself into the ancient nook that had been built for it. As the door tucked itself away, the light it carried faded.

"We've no lantern nor sphinx light," Eleanor murmured, but a smile slanted across Mallory's mouth. He withdrew the pouch she had gifted him with earlier, and dumped the trio of golden nutmegs into his hand.

"If the lady wouldn't take offense, this paint might burn," Mallory said. He stepped into the darkened tomb, still seeing better than Eleanor in such surroundings.

"You would burn your wish for a prosperous and rich new year, Mallory?" she asked from the doorway, trying to see into the gloom. She couldn't even pick out Mallory's shadow, though she heard his steps—a hard floor, dusted with sand here and there.

"My year is already rich, Eleanor," he said. "I would burn this wish so we might see—ooof—this tomb, yes—ah, clever bloody Egyptians. This should do—shield your eyes."

Eleanor wasn't expecting the flame that burst from Mallory's position; it wasn't nutmegs burning, she knew that much, for there was too much light, too much fire. Beneath the edge of her hand, she saw the standing sconce he'd found, and beneath that, an amphorae of what was likely oil. Around the sconce, a ring of hammered metal disks threw the light up, toward the ceiling, where other disks sent the light flooding back down. The chamber filled with a light that called to mind the last gasps of a sunset, before the sun was swallowed by night.

Mallory returned the nutmegs to his pocket as Eleanor stepped into the chamber. The room was a perfect rectangle, six columns preventing to the shale ceiling from collapsing. The columns had once been painted, but time had eaten the color away, leaving only the hieroglyphs behind. Blue paint clung yet to the ceiling, in rough patches that held also golden stars. Eleanor stepped through the columns and drew herself up short. In the center of the space there stood an elevated stone platform, holding not a sarcophagus, but a body.

Her work involved a good many dead bodies—countless mummies wrapped and buried and carefully labeled—but this body was more akin to the bones she had seen in the Paris catacombs. No sarcophagus, and while the skin was withered and brown as if mummified, every inch of it had been wrapped in what looked like translucent silk. The arms and legs were in turn wrapped with jewels; necklaces poured from every limb, and gold and gemstone rings adorned every toe and finger bone. The skull was also wrapped in silk and gems, elaborate strands of lapis and gold overflowing the head as hair might have once.

Strangest of all—though Eleanor allowed the entire setting was strange—a clumsy crook and flail had been placed in the hands, crossed over the chest. It was exactly as one would find a pharaoh, the symbols of their office held close even in death.

"*Mon Dieu,*" Mallory whispered, and his shadow flickered as he crossed himself. "Eleanor—is..." He circled the elevated platform, eyes never leaving the body. "Is it a pharaoh?"

Eleanor pulled her gaze away, the body nearly more disturbing than fascinating. She circled the platform, not daring to touch it. She didn't want to touch a thing within the tomb, so bothersome was the body. But the platform was not marked, lending no clue to the body's identity. She looked to the columns and walls next, finding some relief in the discover

75

of a story upon the columns.

"Not a pharaoh," Eleanor said softly, trying to piece the puzzle together. "There was belief he should have been, however. He was killed before time could take its proper course." She touched the column then, her finger tracing the same name she had found within her father's journal. It was wrapped within a cartouche, exactly as it would be had he been a royal. "Imiut."

She looked back at the body, at the young man's face beyond the silk shroud. He looked wholly at peace, but somewhere his body would give evidence to the wound that had claimed his young life. Or perhaps it had been poison, rotting him from the inside.

"Eleanor."

At the sound of Mallory's voice, she looked to find him beside another of the columns on the other side of the body. He tapped the stone and its hieroglyphs. "Come see this—it's familiar, but I don't know why. I can't read this."

Eleanor rounded the platform to join Mallory at the column. She had no expectations for what she might find—given the tomb and its body, it might have been anything, so the writing beside Mallory's hand startled her as badly as the body had.

"Why do I know this?" Mallory asked.

Tears blurred Eleanor's vision and she shook her head. "You know that, Mallory, because the same mark was on Hatshepsut's temple. It's my grandmother's name, Sagira el Jabari. The Queen of the Mirror." Her grandmother's cartouche was surmounted by an image of Anubis, holding a darkened ankh in his hand. Eleanor didn't like it one bit. Nearby was a mark of Nephthys, Anubis' own mother.

"Mugabalah knew," Mallory whispered. "Is—was this supposed to be your grandmother's tomb?"

Mention of the sphinx made Eleanor look toward the entry door; she could see the smallest sliver of nooks in the corridor beyond. "A small army of sphinx as protection. A tomb that only two can open." She shook her head. "This tomb was not made *for* my grandmother." To prove her theory, she moved for the walls, running hands over the still-smooth shale. "There should be a door—a way out, because they who built this tomb did not die within it. There would be bones. They left, as surely as we will. Here." Within the wall's hieroglyphs, she felt the knife's edge of a doorway; sealed to be sure, but a passage through which they might leave. And—

"Here." She placed Mallory's hand against the carving, identical to that upon the column. "Sealed by Sagira el Jabari."

Mallory faltered. "She— *Made* this tomb?"

Eleanor shook her head. "The Queen of the Mirror was no worker—an overseer maybe. And certainly she sealed the way," she said softly, admiring the way the oil light moved over Mallory's cheeks. "She saw Imiut to his rest and sealed the way behind her. Her seal will mark the other side of the door, too." She was somehow gratified by the confusion that crossed Mallory's face, the way he shook his head and tried to find the words.

"But. That's. Did—? She— *Eleanor.*" Her name was an

explosive whisper in his mouth a second before Mallory kissed her hard. "Do you think— Is it possible— Your father— Is—" Mallory laughed and shook his head.

Eleanor pulled Mallory to the ground so they might sit as she pulled out her father's notebook once again. "He does make one mention of Sagira," she said, looking for the page, "but it's seemingly inconsequential—here." Eleanor touched her grandmother's name in her father's hand. "He drew her cartouche—he could have seen it at Deir el-Bahri as we did, wanted to bring it with him for comparison. But he also had Imiut's name, Mallory. If my father never set foot in this tomb because he came on his own, how did he have the name?"

"There's another source—a document, a file, a *something*."

"Something he could access because it wasn't this." Eleanor gestured to the room. She felt both exhilarated and nauseated—the idea that this tomb conclusively tied to her lost-in-time grandmother was staggering. Even after all she had learned, the idea that there was more, that there were paths yet to travel, was surprising. She wanted this to be the end point, but rather felt it was the beginning of something entirely new. Yet, it felt familiar—like finding the body of the Lady all over again. "Virgil, can we claim this site? As Mistral agents? I don't want this tomb lost the way the Lady was."

Mallory's hand was warm over Eleanor's; his other arm encircled her, hauling her close. "Yes."

There were no other words then, Eleanor resting against Mallory's chest, calmed by the steady thump of his heart. Lulled by that sound and by countless hours spent underground, Eleanor allowed herself to drift, into an uneasy sleep that was broken by the sound of the tomb door sliding shut. Through the thick columns, she watched a dark figure pass; a figure that smelled of rot and dirt, of marrow and oily fur. As always, the figure grew to a height that filled the space allotted—Eleanor found it amusingly arrogant, for if Anubis could change his size as he liked, the idea that he always had to tower over those before him spoke volumes.

Daughter.

"Anubis," she said.

At her side, Mallory woke and Eleanor gave him a hand up from the floor so they might join the ancient god beside the gem-scattered body. It had not become any less disturbing to Eleanor.

Anubis bowed his head, but it was to the body, not Eleanor and Mallory. The ancient god stood at the feet of the once-young man, his night-black hands spread in a kind of benediction over the dead. Anubis spoke in an ancient tongue that Eleanor only vaguely understood, but his tone was clear, mournful and reverent. When the jackal-headed god finished, he took a step back, to regard Eleanor and Mallory with black eyes.

"Do you know him?" Eleanor asked. Had Anubis wished to visit this chamber himself? If history were anything to go by, Anubis would not have been able to enter the tomb, even with a partner, god-hands ill-formed for working in the modern, mortal world. He and Horus had tried to recover an artifact from the Louvre itself, ending only in the item's partial ruin.

Anubis's ears flicked, brushing the ceiling. "Imiut is a son of Anubis, as you are my daughter. Long ago, his spirit passed through Duat, and was lost to me."

Eleanor thought of her own journey thought Duat—imaginary or not. Had the tomb been made to mirror Imiut's journey? Hallways that were once solid, shimmering away; an underworld that could not be explained, a host of horrors, and absolutely the sense of being lost to the real world, trapped under the weight of the world.

"As my emissary, Sagira sealed his body away—assuring me none would solve the riddle of the tomb, that time would protect him even as I could not. Time has proven adequate until now—until gifts of the new year exchange hands, until one curious granddaughter who also possesses the power of my blood."

Perhaps Eleanor should have blushed or felt shame, but she didn't. She stood a little taller, taking it as praise—if none had solved the tomb's riddle before them? She considered that high praise, indeed.

"It's surprising robbers didn't find the tomb," Mallory said, "though given the nature of their greed...even a pair of robbers would have betrayed each other before reaching this chamber."

"So it has been," Anubis said, and Eleanor thought of the bones they found in the first corridor. He reached for the ankh within her hold and gently pulled it away. It looked more proper in his hand, a weapon and instrument both. "I shall prepare the way, Daughter."

Anubis brushed past them, through the columns and to the far wall where Eleanor had found the door's seam. The hands of a god were largely clumsy in this world, though in this instance destruction suited them well; Anubis broke the door from the wall, the crumbling shale revealing Sagira's mark on the opposite site as Eleanor predicted it would. She paused to touch the mark, already knowing she wanted it back in her workshop; she wanted it in the archive, where she could study it. Where, she admitted to herself, she could keep some part of her grandmother's world nearby.

Beyond the door lay a rubble strewn corridor, as dark as any they had already encountered. Eleanor and Mallory managed to fashion a clumsy torch with his torn shirt and the shovel, lighting it with the fire that still burned in the standing sconce. When at last they broke through the final doorway, moving it together as they had every other door in the tomb, the sky was impossibly bright and large; Eleanor was sure the sky had never been that size, shaded as a fresh, ripe peach. She dragged in a deep breath of air; air that was not rotten with death or dust; air that made her feel as if she were breathing for the first time ever. At her side, Mallory did the same and tossed the lousy torch to the ground.

"Damnation!"

From behind them, a raucous cry. They turned as one, finding Gin running toward them. They had emerged not far from the airship's original anchor point, the tomb entry swarming with other agents.

"Eleven days!" Gin cried. "Eleven days and you—You—"

The pilot flung himself at Eleanor and Mallory, sweeping them both into a fierce hug. Behind him, a host of agents, each trying their best to budge the main tomb door. Among them stood Cleo Barclay and Michael Auberon, who looked with no small measure of relief at Gin's commotion.

"Eleven—" Mallory pushed away from their pilot and fellow agent.

"Eleven days—sealed like a snail in its shell. We haven't been able to move the door and here you come, out the back end, like it ain't no big concern." Gin glanced into the hole they'd climbed out of and shuddered. "Spiders down there? Big bloody—" He broke off at the sight of Mallory's ruined, and now missing, clothing. "Shirt-consuming spiders..."

Eleanor moved past them, headed toward Cleo. The agent greeted her with a warm hug, expressing dismay over their eleven-day absence. Eleanor didn't want to think about it—how long they had wandered in Duat, how long it had been since they seen the actual sky.

"You won't believe it," Eleanor said, "what's down there. We need to organize a team."

Cleo tilted her head. "Not plundered?"

Eleanor couldn't dwindle the discovery to a single word. "That doesn't begin to cover it," she said with a grin.

VI.

Eleanor sank into the bathtub, hot water up to her chin, closing her eyes to revel in the warmth. And the clean. If she and Mallory had truly been in the tomb for eleven days, she could only imagine how awful she must smell beyond even the guano they'd been splattered in. Mallory hadn't complained, but then he was a wolf—she supposed he'd rolled around in much fouler scents, and this made her laugh, her breath disturbing the water. She would not think of what she, as a jackal, had rolled in, no.

It was odd, that—eleven days. While Eleanor emerged hungry and thirsty, it wasn't eleven days worth of either. Neither had her body had any complaints that it likely should have after such a time. But how many days had they walked in Duat, if it had indeed been the underworld? Perhaps time had a way of passing differently there. When one was dead, did time pass? Had they been dead?

She thought again of the young body within the tomb, of the gems that carefully covered him and the crook and flail in his hands. If he hadn't been a pharaoh, they had surely treated him as such. A son of Anubis—able to change his form as Anubis and Eleanor did, into a sleek jackal. He had been buried with love and respect, by Eleanor's own grandmother. She pictured Sagira on her knees, making her mark upon the tomb door once it had been sealed for eternity.

"Folley." A gentle knock at the door adjoining her room to Mallory's sounded.

"It's unlocked, Virgil," she called, not moving from the tub. Not opening her eyes.

She listened as Mallory approached, trying to gauge where he was from sound alone—an exercise they had practiced many times in their animal forms. The door whispered shut and Mallory's firm steps sounded across the hardwood floor. He paused, perhaps glancing around the sitting room, before he angled himself toward the bathroom. There was a screen between the door and tub, but even so, Eleanor heard the way he sucked in his breath.

"Miss Folley."

Eleanor smiled, opening her eyes to peer at him through the sheer fabric that screened him from her. "You've seen me in much less than water." She reached out to grasp the edge of the screen and push its first panel gently to the side so she could see him framed in the doorway. His cheeks did not burn with blush, but his eyes were deeply gold, intent on her as she leaned an arm against the edge of the tub. "You smell like lotuses." He smelled like other things, too—whiskey, desire, and the ever-present Egyptian dust that hung in the air, even inside.

A low bench occupied the wall opposite the tub and Mallory sank onto its padded surface. "You do not," he said, mouth edging into a slow smile. "They're bringing food up, if you're hungry."

"I could eat," Eleanor said, and realized then for the first time how hungry she actually was. "Any reports?"

They'd come back to the hotel after Auberon and Cleo

assured them they would secure the tomb for overnight; the following day, they meant to return with a crew. With cameras, and tools, and boxes. Eleanor almost didn't want to move the mummy, but knew it wasn't safe where it was. It was possible word of the tomb and its riches was already spreading, and Mistral would have to move quickly to ensure its contents were preserved.

"Director Hassan has two teams stationed at the tomb overnight," Mallory said. "Both entries covered—though the first remains closed and I've not told them how to open it."

The path his eyes tracked over Eleanor's shoulder and down her arm was nearly palpable. She shivered and drew her arm back into the warmth of the bathwater. A silver tray spread the width of the tub's foot, holding a variety of cloths, soaps, and oils. Eleanor sat up enough to grab a washcloth and an oval of hard soap that was redolent with honey and cream. She offered them to Mallory.

"Scrub my back?"

Mallory unbuttoned his cuffs, to roll his sleeves up to his elbows. Every single move was deliberate: the way he turned the linen back and didn't simply crumple it up, the way he slid to a knee upon the tiled floor and leaned in to claim the soap and washcloth from her. Eleanor wasn't remotely cold under his warming gaze. Strands of Eleanor's hair had escaped her hasty chignon and Mallory brushed these gently away before dunking soap and cloth into the water.

"Do you think we were gone eleven days, Virgil?" Eleanor sat straighter, drawing her knees up into her chest and wrapping her arms around them. Mallory drew progressively harder circles on her back, working out every knot as he went; Eleanor thought she might melt and slide down the drain.

"It didn't even feel like two," he said, drawing the washcloth down her spine and back up again. "Gin has been more than a little concerned—it won't surprise me if he's the one who brings our food up, he'll hardly let me leave his sight."

"Do you think we'll be able to reach it again—Duat, or whatever we may call it?" Mallory dunked the washcloth into the bath, then drew it over Eleanor's back, squeezing the cloth empty. Rivulets of water slid around Eleanor, over the curve of her breast, but before she grew cold, Mallory's bare hand brushed the water away. The warmth of him against her wet back erased everything.

"We'll map the way," he said, kissing away the droplets of water that covered Eleanor's left shoulder as his hand slid more firmly around her. "I think, without the portal into Duat, that tomb is of a very ordinary size. Maybe the two stone paths connect—everything within that tomb required two, Eleanor, so why not two paths that are actually one."

Eleanor turned as Mallory's head came up, to meet his mouth with her own. He tasted like Irish whiskey and Eleanor drank him down. He had not shaved, but neither had his beard shown any sign of going untended for eleven days. Eleanor took a long taste of him, groaning soft into his mouth when his thumb brushed hard across her nipple. Two paths that were actually one, she thought. Two paths that were—

"Virgil."

She murmured his name and tried to pull back, but Mallory slid closer, careless of the way her wet body pressed against his fresh shirt and vest, careless of the way the bathwater sloshed against the side of the tub and onto him. Eleanor broke her mouth away, but Mallory's mouth kissed and bit an insistent, determined line down the column of her neck, into her collarbone. A soft cry broke from her mouth and she slid her hand into his hair. She made a fist of it and pulled him back.

"Virgil."

She felt as intoxicated as he looked when she met his gaze. He was breathing hard, his mouth forming into a little snarl as she stared at his well-kissed mouth.

"El—"

"Two paths, you said," she whispered. "Two paths that are actually one." Eleanor untangled her hand from Mallory's hair, to slide onto her knees and turn to face him. Bathwater poured from her body, lapping around her thighs. "Virgil—we could not have—"

Mallory's hand closed back over Eleanor's bared breast and she sucked in a hard breath. She covered his hand with her own and he did not move, though very much looked as though he meant to.

"One door we opened," Eleanor said, "and one door we never could have—the way it was sealed? There were no mechanisms when Anubis broke it down." Her skin was running to gooseflesh but it was not the temperature in the room that caused it to do so. It was the very idea that—

That—

"Are you telling me that—" Mallory's eyes cleared some, but he did not lift his hand from Eleanor. "Someone wanted us there?"

"We never would have gotten out without Anubis," Eleanor said. "We couldn't have gone back—the way was shut, all those traps. And the way forward was—" She thought of her grandmother's mark upon the columns, upon the door, but also Anubis's own image—a son of Anubis buried within the tomb. "And *he* couldn't have gotten *in* without *us*. Couldn't have gotten the ankh without us."

Something akin to heartache washed over Mallory's face; Eleanor felt her own stomach sink, as though she would be sick. A god's hands were clumsy in this world, she thought, as Mallory gave her a hand out of the tub and wrapped her into her robe. They had learned directly the way a god's hands worked in the modern world; where once they had power, the ancient gods had no such thing now; they could reach through a glass case, but could not withdraw a treasure without causing damage to both it and the case. Mallory pressed a hard kiss against her forehead.

"I have to reach Director Hassan."

Mallory moved away from Eleanor, striding from the bath, but she was hard on his heels. "Mallory, if it *is* Anubis, Hassan stands no hope of stopping him. If Anubis wanted to reclaim one of his own—" Eleanor shuddered. "How long has it been? The tomb could already be empty."

They made swift work of dressing and bypassed a tray-laden Gin in the hallway. Eleanor briefly mourned the idea of dinner—it would be cold by the time they returned—but Gin kept the trays in hand, even as he turned to follow them. *The Jackal* was ready to fly, and as Gin lifted them into the night sky yet again, Eleanor and Mallory devoured the dinner— tender hand pies oozing with lamb, gravy and vegetables, wrapped in a buttery crust. With food in her, Eleanor felt more steady by the time the airship skimmed over Deir el-Bahri, but as they touched down, and ran toward the new tomb, she saw they were too late. Miss Wise and Mister Gathright were no longer at their posts, sprawled instead upon the ground some distance away. The other team of recruits were likewise, all unconscious, yet breathing still.

With lamps and revolvers, they plunged back into the tomb via the secondary entrance Anubis had broken open, this time with Gin and a host of other agents at their backs. The rubble strewn corridor seemed worse this time and Eleanor wasn't certain if it was because they were so frantic to reach the burial chamber—but when her boot came down on something metal, and cracked it wide open, her heart lodged in her throat. Scattered down the entire corridor were the remains of destroyed sphinxes. None had been spared, bodies flung from end to end; at the chamber's broken doorway, blood colored the threshold, and within its crimson flood, footprints. The sphinx, Eleanor thought, had tried to fight the intruder off. Had tried to fight *Anubis* off.

Mallory shouldered his way into the columned room, where more sphinx lay dead and dismembered. And beyond the columns, upon the platform where a jeweled body once lay— Only the faintest impression of the body remained, an outline in the softest tomb dust, as if it had been plucked up like a sleeping child, and carried to proper bed.

From the corridor beyond, there came a terrible snarling and when Eleanor shined her lantern within, she was not surprised to discover actual jackals prowling in the darkness. They bristled at the sight of her, fanged mouths bared in snarls. Jackals and the dead went hand in hand, didn't they. A clumsy god's hands, she thought, and growled angrily at the jackals, feeling her own jackal very close to the surface. She wanted to let it loose, wanted to chase them into the night, and scream at the moon; she did not. The desert jackals bolted past her, tails tucked as they fled up the corridor and out the tomb, into the desert night. Eleanor sank against the doorway, watching Mallory and Gin stalk through the columns. But she knew they wouldn't find anything—Anubis would have taken it.

"Eleanor."

At the sound of Mallory's voice, she came to his side, startled at what his lantern light illuminated. In the fine dust and sand upon the floor, there sat a strand of lapis beads and beside them, a ring. It was simple, a single thin band of gold that Eleanor would have known anywhere. She didn't want to touch it, but scooped it from the sand nonetheless. Eleanor straightened, holding the ring as one might something that had rotten and gone foul.

"It's Irish gold, Mallory," she said. "It's my mother's." She offered her revolver and the ring to Mallory, who took them without a word, sliding the ring into his pocket. As he did, Eleanor stalked out of the room, up the debris-choked corridor, and into the night where she felt the cooling air on her damp cheeks.

"Anubis!"

She screamed his name to the star-spattered sky over and over, but it was the dark ground that spat him up, a body coalescing from the sand itself. The darkest parts of the desert became the ancient god and he towered above Eleanor, as if his bulk could intimidate her. She did not back down, snarling at him as sand poured from his shoulders, down his thighs.

"We had an agreement," Eleanor said, hands closed into fists. The jackal within her bristled beneath her skin, but she refused to give it ground; becoming the jackal meant losing her words, and it was her words Anubis needed to hear. "I may carry your blood and may be called *daughter*, but I am my own person! You used me. You used *us*. To reach that chamber. To reach that body."

"*That was no mere body.*"

Anubis roared the words and it was as though the world had come apart. Eleanor's vision blurred with tears, and flying sand corrupted it further. She could not see and could not breathe. She thought she was still screaming, her throat gone raw, and she stumbled against the hard wind; she went down to her knees, hands fisting into the sand in an effort to hold on.

"*Beloved of the queen, beloved of the daughter,*" Anubis roared anew. "*My eternal blood.*"

She could not see, but rather felt Anubis's departure. The

sand ceased its whirlwind, falling as abruptly as it had lifted; the fury went out of the sky and took Anubis with it. Eleanor could breathe again, ragged gulps that left her shaking. She felt Mallory at her back, hauling her from the sand and into his arms, and watched Gin running circles around them, guns raised as if he meant to do the god harm should he return.

But Anubis did not return, and the desert was as still as death itself, growing colder as the night deepened.

What could not be taken from the tomb were the walls and their markings; Eleanor held to this as she brushed her hair before bed. The Mistral recruits had woken without incident—they'd felt sick, and passed out, but felt better once roused and given water, and insisted on standing their shifts. It would be a quiet night, Eleanor knew.

But of the tomb, there were still hieroglyphs to read and translate; there were still passageways to explore and ponder. It would be as any other robbed tomb, Eleanor told herself as she set her brush aside. Not that any other tomb had held a body wearing her mother's wedding ring. She felt sickened by the very idea. Eleanor rose from the vanity and crossed to the bed where Mallory already sprawled against the pillows, reading her father's journal.

"New revelations?"

"Not a blessed thing," he said, and closed the small book. He set it on the bedside table as Eleanor slipped beneath the covers and tucked herself into his side.

"I'm not going to ask him, Virgil," she said. "My father. It's plain he knew the tomb connected to my mother—to

Sagira. If not their resting place, then a place they had a connection to. Given how far back my mother travelled...I hope she lived a long life, a life that saw her doing what she always dreamed of. He never said a word, and— Well. Asked me to give my search up, when even he could not."

Mallory smoothed a hand over Eleanor's hair, letting the silence run between them. There were so many questions, Eleanor felt they might flood the room, but they each left them unasked.

"And I think..." Eleanor exhaled, beginning to unbutton Mallory's silken nightshirt. The shirt topped a pair of loose, draw-string pants; Eleanor approved wholeheartedly of it, for it was easy to undo. "I said I would be done—chasing my mother's ghost?" She propped herself up on an elbow in order to better undo the buttons. When they had all been loosened, Eleanor bent to press a kiss against Mallory's bared chest. "I think ghosts are part of the business, aren't they? We open these ancient spaces and they're still inhabited. Every place is haunted."

Eleanor sat up, to push the shirt off Mallory's shoulders; he sat up to help, but drew her into his lap as soon as the shirt was gone. Eleanor straddled him, her nightgown hitching up her thighs, her fingers threading into his hair as she kissed him. Long and slow, as if she'd never kissed him before. Eleanor took her time, enjoying the way Mallory's eyes shut and the way he did not exactly relax, but the way the tension still escaped him. As if she could swallow it all and carry it away. He did the same for her, for as the kiss deepened and he unbuttoned the pearl buttons at the bodice of her nightgown, she felt him stripping every bit of worry from her mind.

"No place has to be," Mallory said, his mouth having trailed to Eleanor's jaw, to the narrow silk ribbon which tied the neck of her nightgown closed. He licked the ribbon into his mouth and gave it a firm tug with his teeth. As the cotton and lace parted, Mallory's eyes met hers. "We can banish every ghost that haunts you—the way we've begun to banish mine."

Eleanor had felt ridiculous in the nightgown, had called herself foolish for packing it at all, but with Mallory staring at her the way he was—his eyes shimmering gold and brown, the end of her ribbon caught at the corner of his mouth—she felt ridiculous no more. She was loved and respected, and above all else, valued. She twisted her finger into the ribbon and gently tugged it from Mallory's mouth, shrugging out of the nightgown until it pooled around her waist. Mallory's breath stuttered then and she leaned down, rubbing her nose against his.

"We ride it out," she said.

Mallory echoed the words—as she had done months before in the wreck of an airship in the desert dark—but only once he had tumbled Eleanor into the pillows, and kissed her until she could not breathe evenly. Until she was well and thoroughly ravished—and had ravished well and thoroughly in return—and wanted only to sleep. But even then, Mallory curled around her from behind, whispering in her ear, keeping her from drifting.

"Tell me, then," Mallory said, his hand splaying against her chest until she was certain he could feel the beat of her heart. "Three nutmegs alone?"

Eleanor laughed, covering Mallory's hand with her own. "You find my innocent gift suspicious?" Mallory's teeth pressed gently into Eleanor's shoulder, until she squirmed in pleasure and twisted in his hold to face him. In the dark, his eyes were wide, fathomless. There was no single reason she loved him, nor he her; it was a ceaseless circle in her thoughts, much as the tomb they had walked.

"There is nothing innocent about you or nutmegs." He dropped a kiss onto her nose and Eleanor closed her eyes, nodding.

"It's true." When Mallory said no more, she suspected he'd fallen asleep, though when she looked at him again, he was watching her, as still as a wolf in the woods. "I've another gift for you, it's also true." Her bare feet tangled with his as she slid a leg over him to pull him closer. "It will require travel, and tea, and courage, Mallory," she said in the most serious voice she could muster. "A willingness to meet ghosts and perhaps slay them."

An eyebrow went up. "We possess each in full measure, did we not agree?"

Eleanor made a soft noise and slipped from the bed, surprised Mallory didn't hold her right where she was. But she was aware of the weight of his eyes upon her as she padded, naked and sure, toward her luggage. From its depths, she drew an envelope, and brought it back to the bed for Mallory. As he fumbled with the wax seal, Eleanor crawled back into the bed. Would it be amusing, or terrible, the thing she had given him?

There was the rustle of the paper coming open. The crinkle of spreading it flat.

"Eleanor—"

"Yes, Mallory."

"—a tomb?"

Eleanor's mouth split in a grin. "An Irish *megalithic* tomb—parts of which *might* be quite related to Egyptian architecture, *and* Mayan!"

The paper rustled again and then Mallory was pulling her down into the rumpled pillows, into the warmth of the nest they had made there. Eleanor was no longer quite alarmed at the way her body responded to him, to his closeness or his touch, but neither was she entirely calm when he kissed her breathless once more. He pulled her down and down, where he tasted like forever, and his hands hardly shook at all, not when he was holding her.

"You will be the death of me, Eleanor Folley."

"Yes, Mallory."

Acknowledgements

I place mysterious tombs right up there with haunted houses when I rank strange places I love. I knew Folley and Mallory would have to get into tomb trouble sooner or later and though I took a few liberties with Egyptian tomb design, I hope they were enjoyed.

To Indiana Jones, who taught me important lessons about raiding tombs: namely, don't, because people want their things, hey why are they chasing you, maybe you took their *thing*. To Lara Croft, for the hours and hours (and hours) spent running through temples and tombs and pyramids, fighting off mummies and gods. To Amelia Peabody (and Elizabeth Peters), who took me around Egypt every digging season. To Adele Blanc-Sec, who ventured into tombs and strange places without flinching. To Vanessa Ives, who did the same.

To my readers, be it first draft or last: Jennifer Kahng, Anna C. Bowling, James Gathright, Patt Castro, and Aidan Doyle. To all those who've stayed the course and helped me with a little bit of this and a little bit of that, whether they know it or not: A. C. Wise, Dean Smith-Richard, Scott Andrews, Julia Rios, Neil Clarke, Sunny Moraine, Alex Acks, Molly Tanzer, Alexis Hunter, and the extraordinary Wendy Wagner. And, to the spoon-shaped muse, because tombs navigated at a distance are no less present.

Folley and Mallory will return in *The Quartered Heart*.

BIOGRAPHY

E. Catherine Tobler is a Sturgeon Award finalist, the senior editor at *Shimmer Magazine*, and a cupcake connoisseur. Among others, her short fiction has appeared in *Clarkesworld*, *Lightspeed*, and *Lady Churchill's Rosebud Wristlet*. For more, visit ecatherine.com

The Thing In The Ice

In the vast, black emptiness between Mars and Jupiter, Ceres was melting

Buried within the asteroid's core, Ceres Station provides water-ice for an ever-growing system of corporations and explorers, each intent on carving their names into the future of the galaxy. But no one anticipates the secret Ceres harbors.

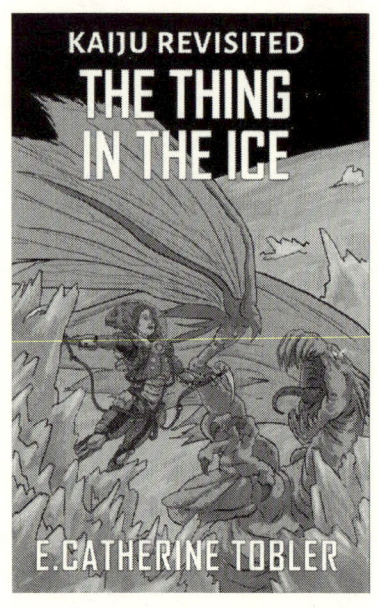

Ice cutter Flit Navarro knows how to haul ice from asteroids and that Scrabble boards only have six Rs. She's never confronted mercenaries intent on claiming Ceres Station for themselves. She's never plummeted to the lowest levels of the station to confront a secret waking from the ice, a monster of ice and instinct.

But she's about to.

apokrupha.com/the-thing-in-the-ice

Home Birth

The largest and most hostile creature in the galaxy needs an heir.

Eibal has grown embryos for nearly every species in the galactic web. As a "sympathetic genetic," she and her crew provide procreation services to infertile creatures like the gentle yaerla, the star-sea kreb, and the third most aggressive race in the galaxy, human beings.

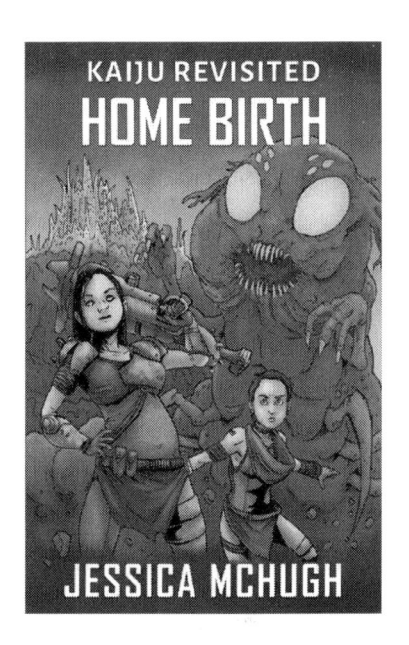

When the queen of the darkogs makes Eibal an offer she can't refuse, she and her partner Naka risk everything to give her an heir. But few places in the galaxy are more dangerous than the darkog kingdom of the Southern Ring, and Eibal soon finds herself entrenched in a brutal war between humans, darkogs, and her own body.

apokrupha.com/home-birth

Manufactured by Amazon.ca
Bolton, ON

35171933R00062